NAME NOT GIVEN

A JACK WIDOW THRILLER

SCOTT BLADE

Black Lion Media

PUBLISHED BY BLACK LION MEDIA.

ALSO BY SCOTT BLADE

1

I STARED at a dead woman on a cold metal table, not a slab, like in the movies, but a table.

In the movies, the dead woman was usually played by an actress. Usually, she would be naked or covered up with a clean white sheet. She would be a live person, pretending to be dead. She would be painted in white makeup to make her look lifeless.

This was no actress. Nothing looked fake. No white makeup painted on her. There were no prosthetic scars or fake bruises or rubbery black eyes.

The woman I looked at was very dead.

In life, her name had been Karen Dekker.

Someone murdered her. But first, they had beaten her nearly to death with a hammer.

The FBI had arrested a guy. They arrested him for killing three other women.

He was in jail for it. He was on death row for it.

But the person who killed her wasn't the same guy they had on death row, which made people doubt that the guy they had arrested nearly two years earlier for a series of similar murders was guilty.

How could he kill Karen Dekker if he were locked up?

The guy that they had on death row had been convicted of killing a series of women, in the same manner, hammer and all, following the same MO—torturing them in the same ways. And all for the same apparent reason—military desertion.

He had killed a series of women because they had all supposedly gone AWOL.

AWOL means absent without leave. The military loves acronyms, even for slang.

Actually, AWOL doesn't mean exactly that. The dictionary definition is absent without intent to desert. However, that's not what most people think. Most people think it means to abandon your post, intentionally and intending to desert the Army.

Like most of the world, the guy they had arrested for the murders also thought it meant to desert.

The guy who sat on death row had less than sixty-one hours to go. He was a dead man walking.

Karen Dekker's broken body was bruised and blunted and pulped, nearly beyond recognition.

As I stared over her, I noted her captor hadn't bothered to restrain her arms. And he hadn't bothered because he had broken them both at the elbows—no need to tie her up. Her bashed, shattered elbows had made fighting back impossible.

I stopped looking over her for a moment and closed my eyes. I imagined the killer. I tried to put myself in his shoes. I tried to forget who I was, that I was a good guy. I tried to think like a depraved murderer, which I could do easily enough. All it took was empathy and an active imagination. Luckily, I had both.

I imagined all the horrible, gut-wrenching things that the

killer could've done to her with a hammer. A surplus of gruesome images flashed through my brain. I imagine my facial expressions winced in response to each of them, but I kept my eyes shut. I watched them all.

Finally, I opened my eyes and stared back down at her. I ticked off each of the horrifying acts I had imagined an insane psycho could do. Not one of the horrible things on my list had been missed by this killer. He had done just about everything sickening that a man could do with a hammer and a helpless kidnapped victim.

It was all out of a bad nightmare.

The killer had used the hammer to shatter her elbows, bust her kneecaps, pulverize her toes into mush, and pummel her lower face and jaw to pulp.

It looked like most of her bones in her arms and legs were crushed to sawdust under the skin.

Dekker's teeth were gone from her mouth. But they were in the room with us.

They were trodden and shattered into cracked, small pieces and souped into a tin bowl next to her head.

Her body had been found in the water. She had washed up onshore. Which made me wonder how they found her teeth. So, I asked the medical examiner who was just an Army physician.

I asked, "She was washed up by the tide?"

"Right," he said.

"Where did you find her teeth?"

"They were in her mouth."

"They looked like they were bashed out?"

"The killer stuffed them back in her mouth."

I recoiled and said, "He put them back?"

"Looks that way."

"Why?"

The doctor shrugged.

"Guess he wanted to make sure that we could identify her."

"Why?" I asked again.

Again, he shrugged.

The killer had smashed her teeth apart, and the medical examiner had put them out for us to see. I didn't ask why he displayed them like that because I figured it was SOP for Army doctors.

Like the Navy and the Marines, the Army had detailed instruction manuals for everything. I imagined that somewhere, written in some manual, was that if human teeth were found separate from a murdered body, they were required to be collected and displayed for the investigators to see.

Despite the enormous damage that the killer had done to this poor woman, he had left her forehead and scalp unscathed. The skin above her eyebrows was undamaged, as was her hair—all except for the damage by seawater and the Atlantic currents.

The killer had stopped at her eyes and nose.

I didn't have to ask the doctor why. I knew why.

He had done this because he didn't want to kill her with the hammer. He had wanted her to stay alive. He wanted her to know how she was going to die. He wanted her to feel it.

I felt my stomach wrench at the sight of her.

I never knew Karen Dekker. She had been a soldier, and I had been a Navy SEAL, but she was still my sister. We were still a part of the military family. All soldiers were my family; the same goes for Marines, airmen and sailors.

I tried to ignore the intense pain that Dekker had endured for a moment. And I focused on the question of how?

How could someone lure her onto a boat and to her death like that?

I imagined the kinds of scenarios that would require her to be tricked. The possibilities were endless, but essentially the gist of them all boiled down to two basic possibilities.

She either knew the killer, trusted him, and allowed herself to be vulnerable. Or she had been abducted against her will. Probably at gunpoint. It was most likely the latter was the case.

That was how all the other women had been murdered.

I opened my eyes again.

The Army doctor had been standing there with me and one of the FBI agents that I came with.

The doctor had been speaking, talking to the FBI agent, ignoring me.

He had described the killing, like a Shakespearean student who stayed up all night studying a monologue. Now, he was reciting it to us. I didn't care about most of what he was saying. I tuned it out until he said, "Her assailant pounded on her elbows, shattering the bones."

No shit, I thought.

I closed my eyes and imagined a blacksmith hammering smoldering metal on an anvil. I imagined him waling away at it, bending and shaping it into the desired specifications of the object that he was creating. I imagined the sparks flying and spraying into tiny particles of dust and fire.

But the killer hadn't been a blacksmith. Blacksmiths created things. This killer wasn't creating but subduing, demolishing a person's life.

Both of her arms were stretched out and laid by her sides as natural as they could've been. And they still looked awkward, like a mangled plastic mannequin.

They had told me she was found on a more remote part of Cocoa Beach, a point that was still used for surfing by the locals, but she had floated there for up to twenty-four hours before she was found.

Her body had been washed up after a storm. A storm that I had also been in.

It turned out that she had been found this morning only three miles from where I had been standing, twenty-four hours ago, on a deserted beach.

Dekker had been killed by a high-velocity nine-millimeter bullet that burst through her head and ricocheted around in her brainpan, ripping through tissue and cracking the inside of her skull.

Three days earlier, Army Corporal Karen Dekker had gone missing from the Cocoa Beach area. One minute she had been there, and the next, she was gone. She had been a surfer, like me. I would say that she was much more into it than I was. I had only done it recreationally, maybe once or twice a year. According to her friends, Dekker had seen it as a way of life.

On the last day that anyone had seen her alive, she had gone out to surf, alone. Apparently, that hadn't been that unusual for her.

However, she was known for being a true professional soldier. She never missed a day of work. She always called if she had to be away—that sort of thing.

But the day she went surfing, she never returned home. The next morning she didn't show up at work.

After she was deemed missing, the Army MPs searched for her. It was a short-lived search. A major mistake by the Army.

They immediately jumped the gun.

Within a few days, they believed she had gone AWOL. The MPs' reasoning behind this was because there evidence that she wasn't happy about her new assignment.

She had been stationed in South Florida and loved it. But now they took that away from her.

She had been given an assignment to return to a tour in Iraq. As a part of the first all-women combat convoy to enter ISIS-controlled areas.

The whole thing sounded like a PR act of desperation by the Army. I figured Dekker saw this too. She probably was insulted by it.

They say that wars are fought and won at home, not out in the war zones.

One difference between the Army and the Navy is the culture of the generals versus that of the Navy's admirals.

Every admiral that I've ever met had been a certified history buff. It is a part of their fraternity, like how college professors sit around and argue about theories that no one else cares about. Admirals and generals argue about battle tactics. Truly this was an example of elitism at its best.

Like the admirals I knew, Army generals were also war history buffs, but they celebrated land wars and long-dead Army generals and philosophers of war, whereas admirals talked about sea warfare and old stories of famous ships and captains.

One philosopher that they both shared in terms of Warfare 101 was Machiavelli.

Good old Machiavelli said that appearances were everything. Wars are won in public opinion, not in body count or bombs dropped, or land was taken. If the American public supports a war, then they'll support the victory. But if they don't support a war, then it's already lost.

Things aren't always what they appear.

On the surface, it appeared that Dekker abandoned her post.

She had already spent two tours in Iraq, way back during

the height of the war. Once she returned stateside, she was quite vocal against it.

I had learned that she wasn't willing to go back. She desperately tried to get out of orders to return to the Middle East a few times. She had even written all over her social media her distaste for our current deployments in the Middle East. Not as an ideological thing, but more out of anger that the Army was being wasted there.

I could see her contempt for the politicians in Washington and the four stars in the Pentagon who once had been warriors and now were *glorified pencil-pushers*. Her words. Not mine.

But Karen Dekker never made it to her deployment. She never made it to work. She never even made it home from the beach because she was murdered.

I looked back down at her.

She had two swollen eyes, black, lifeless, but opened, unnaturally opened because they had been beaten shut.

To open them up, the doctor had sliced through the swollen lids right down the middle.

I had asked him why, and he told me it was to see if there was any evidence in them. He was concerned that the killer was playing games. Because of the teeth, I imagined. But there wasn't any evidence in the eye sockets.

The doctor had also mentioned that he had planned to sew them shut before releasing the body to the family for what he called a "proper burial."

The last piece of physical evidence was that there was bruising left behind the ear that showed that the killer had pressed the muzzle of a nine-millimeter handgun back there, and hard too. He had pressed it behind the ear, right side. Then pulled the trigger—a single shot.

This was the only variation from the other dead women. Everything else was the same. Remarkably so.

It was an execution. No doubt.

The doctor said, "He really hated her."

"Why do you say that?"

He stared at me like I was a monster for even asking the question. But the reason I asked was to get his take on it.

"Isn't it obvious? This was done out of hate, out of rage. Look at what he put her through."

I nodded. Still, I wasn't quite convinced. Sure, it looked bad. But there was something calculating about it, like a planned mess.

And there was something else.

I had seen a lot of dead people in my time in the Naval Criminal Investigative Service. I had seen a lot of lifeless corpses and lifeless eyes, but her eyes were different. Something was wrong in them.

I couldn't quite explain it. It was like she had been shocked and surprised by what was coming at her. Which could've been what they all had felt, but this was more. I didn't know what to make of it. Not yet.

Suddenly, I felt a shiver waft over me. We stood in a cold storage room that they had to use as a makeshift morgue because the base didn't have one.

I was in South Florida with an FBI agent who didn't like me all that much.

And I couldn't blame her because I had come along and thrown a wrench into a case that she had closed.

In the last twenty-four hours, I had been on four different flights and in the custody of two different police forces. If you don't count a pair of idiotic beach cops. If you did, then I had been arrested three times, which must have been a record for me.

I stood with the FBI agent and an Army doctor looking over the corpse.

We were on an Army base where I wasn't popular. The day before, they had been putting me in restraints, and now I was back, working with the FBI.

I stepped closer to Dekker's body.

The Army medical doctor stood on the opposite side of the table. He gasped when he saw me reach out and touch the body. Like I was going to check her pulse, second-guessing his assertion that she was dead. I wasn't. I wanted to feel her skin.

I hadn't known Dekker in life, but I wanted to touch her in death. I wanted to touch her because I was feeling rage at what had happened to her, and I wanted to touch her like a family member might brush the hair of a dead relative at a funeral.

It was a second nature thing.

I wore surgical gloves as we all did, but I wasn't authorized to touch her, not in the doctor's eyes. I was an outsider, a nobody. I didn't belong here.

I ignored him and did it, anyway.

Through the glove, I could feel that Dekker was cold, colder than the polished metal table beneath her. She was colder than the ocean water she had washed in on. She might've been colder than the nights in prison, where the guy that they had pegged to be the killer was awaiting death. I wasn't sure if he had murdered the other women or not, but I knew he didn't kill this one.

Even though I had seen dead people before, it had been a long time. I wasn't a cop anymore, and I certainly wasn't military either.

I had been a man who goes everywhere and does anything —attached to nothing. I owed debts to no one. I took orders from no one. I liked it that way.

No one waited up for me. No one waited for me to come home. No one waited to hear where I was or what I was doing. I had no children. No house in the suburbs. No mortgage to pay. No car insurance to worry about. I enjoyed simply living in the moment.

I no longer heard the voice of my team leader in my earpiece telling me when to breach a house or a compound. I no longer heard the WHOP! WHOP! of helicopter blades as I escaped some godforsaken place in the Middle East.

I didn't spend my nights unable to sleep for fear that the enemy would ambush me and kill me while I slept.

I had once been an undercover cop with NCIS. I had been assigned to the SEALs teams. Sometimes my enemies were my friends, and sometimes my friends were my enemies.

Living a double life like that can leave a man not knowing up from down.

That life was far behind me now, and I was glad for it. But this brought me right back into it.

I looked over at the Army doctor and asked, "Any physical evidence that's different with her from the others?"

"Other than the bruise from the muzzle?"

"Other than that?"

The Army doctor said, "It's all in the report, but no. I'd say that her experience was long, drawn-out suffering. Same as the rest. It was bad. She didn't go quickly.

"I've been in the Army for ten years now. I've seen some combat in Iraq. Three tours. And a stretch in Frankfurt. We got a lot of guys there—a lot of hopeless cases. So, I've seen tons of guys flown back from that war. I've seen missing limbs, gunshot wounds, IEDs. You name it. But I've never seen a single soldier endure torture like this."

I stayed quiet.

"Judging by the reports of the other women, this murder syncs up the same. Nothing's different."

I looked at the FBI agent that I had met just twenty hours earlier.

She nodded. There was defeat in her eyes because she knew that this meant her guy wasn't the killer. They had arrested the wrong man.

She said, "It's the same killer."

2

Before I stared at Karen Dekker's broken and bashed and lifeless body, I had been caught up in a temporary setback of my own.

I couldn't breathe!

My first instinct was to open my mouth—wide. Desperately, I wanted to suck in air! I wanted to fill my lungs!

I needed air!

I needed to breathe!

I wanted to gasp a breath of anything!

I was desperate!

But I couldn't breathe!

I couldn't breathe because I was submerged underwater. It had been a sudden shock. I hadn't expected it. Therefore, I hadn't taken a deep breath beforehand.

With all my strength, I fought against the current. My hands and feet propelled and fishtailed and rotored back and forth, out of control, like fragmented helicopter blades.

I was caught in a tailspin.

Lightning cracked and crashed high above. Thunder rumbled and boomed.

The lightning flashed and spider-webbed under the rolling clouds of black.

An hour ago, it hadn't been this bad. An hour ago, the sun beamed across the sky and bounced off fluffy white clouds that floated through the air, soft and harmless.

Everything changed—fast.

Less than a half-hour passed, and suddenly I saw storm clouds roll in over the surface of the ocean. They rolled steadily, foreboding and unstoppable. They had chased away the harmless, fluffy clouds, which I didn't like. And they chased away the tourists, which I did like. They also chased away the local surfers.

But not me. I stayed.

I had seen plenty of bad weather during my time in the Navy. Out on the ocean, surrounded by nothing but endless water and endless sky, the one constant that threatened tranquility was bad weather.

Naval Mariners fought more bad weather than enemy ships at a ratio of a million to one or even ten million to one.

No matter how much time I spent at sea, the weather constantly surprised me. No matter how many times the weather behaved badly, mankind continued to pretend that it was predictable.

Nothing was less predictable than the weather—nothing except for the future.

At the time I was submerged underwater, fighting to breathe, I had no idea about the future and the crimes I was going to get tangled up in.

Being dragged underwater with no breath in my lungs was a little embarrassing because I had once been a sailor and later a Navy SEAL.

I knew how to swim. And I was good at holding my breath.

Guess I shouldn't have been too hard on myself since no one expects to be dragged under by an undertow. If they had, then no one would succumb to them.

Less than a minute earlier, I had been on a rented surfboard. The next moment, I wiped out, and then I was being swept under.

I had lost my footing on the surfboard. That was a split second after I saw the whitecaps grow larger and larger unexpectedly.

I surfed under the storm clouds—my fault.

I was going to turn thirty-six later in the year, and I still acted like I was twenty-six. This was a universal truth that we all go through, a miscalculation of our age and abilities.

Live long enough, and we'll all experienced that moment when we can't quite walk up that long flight of stairs as easily as we once could. We can't run and jump like we could before. We all must start watching our diets one day. We all gotta count calories and watch out for cholesterol. We all will notice that our hair used to be a little thicker, a little less gray.

We all start working a little harder to do the normal things that we used to do so well.

I wasn't there yet. I was only thirty-five years old. But I was closer than I ever had been before—every second ticks down the countdown of our lives.

This wasn't going to be my last tick.

I twisted and heaped and swerved under the ocean like a sea lion caught in a net. Then I frogged my legs back and swam up. At least I hoped it was up.

It turned out it was.

I burst through the waves and gasped for air. I took two deep breaths and held the second one because I knew chances were I was going back under.

This time I had the breath for it. And I had my bearings.

I swam toward the beach.

The next wave passed over me, and I resurfaced. This time I was prepared to stay above the water.

I looked up at the sky. It was a lot darker than I had thought. It looked like the entire atmosphere was one big storm cloud.

I twisted and spiraled around. I was looking for the surfboard. For stupid reasons, I had opted not to fasten the leg rope around my ankle, despite my instinct for safety.

I didn't have a good excuse for not doing it. The best that I could say was that it was like not wearing a seatbelt.

At that moment, I had decided I was too good for it. I had been a SEAL, and I knew how to swim. I was pretty good at it too.

Dumb mistake.

I searched the tops of the crashing waves and saw no sign of the board.

I felt a little frantic about losing it because I had to put a two-hundred-dollar deposit on it. I looked left, looked right. I couldn't see it.

Another heavy wave came rolling at me and crashed over my head. Again, I was swept under, and again, I resurfaced and swam back to shore.

I swam.

It didn't take long because the waves were carrying me half the distance.

Once I made it to the shallow waters, I walked out of the ocean.

The beach was basically deserted, except for a lifeguard truck that was headed in my direction like a security cop with nothing better to do.

Great, I thought. I was in trouble for not getting out earlier.

The truck was a yellow-and-red pickup with a thin light bar mounted on the roof. It flashed red and white. No siren.

I didn't wait around, staring at them. I turned and scanned for the surfboard. No law said that I had to stop and be nice to the local lifeguards. But I wanted to find and return that surfboard.

Two hundred bucks was two hundred bucks.

I was a tall guy, so I didn't have to stretch out or climb up onto anything to see far over the shoreline.

Cocoa Beach was pretty flat, which usually meant a post-card-perfect view, in contrast to the high crashing waves and the blackening, storm-covered skies that had developed this morning.

It was a beautiful beach.

I looked from one side of the coastline to the other. No surfboard. It should've been washed in by the surf. No way did it go out to sea, not in these rough conditions.

I looked out over the ocean. Nothing.

The lifeguard truck was getting closer. The main street was at their backs, and the ocean was at mine. I wouldn't outrun them.

I waited. What choice did I have?

The truck pulled to a stop about ten feet from me. They hadn't been traveling at top speeds, but a truck driving over sand at slow speeds was still going to kick up sand and pebbles as it braked to a stop.

That's exactly what they did. Only they made it all dramatic, like a couple of cops making a bust.

The truck stopped, and I expected two lifeguards to hop out with hands drawn like they were pretend-guns. I expected them to say, "Freeze!"

They did nothing that dramatic or stupid, but they hopped out—fast.

And I had been wrong about them. They weren't lifeguards.

They were beach cops. Technically, they were called Cocoa Beach Police. They were an offshoot of the local police, a beach patrol unit. So they weren't lifeguards, but a fraction of a rung higher than that and a rung lower than bicycle patrol.

Although, I may have been wrong about that because technically, the bicycle patrol has less impressive equipment. They use bicycles and not trucks.

The driver hopped out, shut his door, and adjusted his pants by grabbing his gun belt.

The passenger got out a second later and left his door open. He walked up to the passenger side tire and leaned on the side of the truck and stared at me.

The driver walked down past the hood and the tire and stopped dead in front of the fender.

They had sidearms.

I would be lying if I said that part of me didn't want to laugh out loud.

What were they going to use sidearms for? I imagined that busting a litterbug didn't require guns.

I stayed quiet.

The driver said, "Sir, you got a death wish?"

I didn't answer.

"Sir, did you not see the 'beach closed' sign?"

The passenger said, "Sir, you gonna answer?"

I said, "Is there a law about being on a public beach?"

The driver said, "Sir, this beach is closed. The sign says that very thing. Did you not read it?"

The passenger asked, "Sir, can you read?"

"I can read just fine."

"So, why did you disobey the sign, sir?"

I said, "I didn't see the sign."

"Sir, it's an illegal act to disobey and not to follow the directions of a warning sign in the State of Florida."

"I didn't disobey the sign. I just told you I didn't see it."

The driver said, "Sir, you can spend up to ten nights in jail and pay a fine of one thousand dollars for disobeying a 'beach closed' sign here."

Two hundred bucks, gone. And now a thousand-dollar fine. I was racking up the charges.

The driver moved in closer and moved his right hand, not all the way to his sidearm, but closer to it. I'd say it was in the proximity of it, making it fast to grab, fast enough to draw, which it didn't need to be because I wasn't armed. Not unless I was packing a nine millimeter in my swim trunks.

I wasn't.

"Sir, the fact of the matter is that there is a sign. Not the fact of the matter is that it is irrelevant if you saw it or not."

"Not the fact of the matter," he had said. That was a weird phrase. It made me think that maybe the guy had tried to be clever and tried to come up with something smart to say. A failure on both accounts, but you don't tell that to a guy who has a gun and a legal right to discharge it. Or at least he can discharge it and claim it was under legal circumstances later.

Not something I was interested in being a part of.

I said, "I'm sorry for not reading the sign. My mistake."

The driver stopped walking toward me and gave me a hard look. He looked me up and then down and back up again, which made me feel a little uncomfortable.

He said, "That's some tattoo you got."

The passenger beach cop asked, "How long that takes you to get?"

He was a little younger than the driver. Both beach cops

were about late twenties to early thirties. I could tell in all the obvious ways, but the driver had a middle-aged look about him, like he had been cursed with looking older his whole life.

I knew they weren't really interested in my tattoos. Florida beaches were full of guys with lots of tattoos. Most of America was full of those types of guys now.

I said, "It's not one piece. It's several pieces."

"Huh. They don't come together to form one image?"

"No."

"They look like they were all drawn together."

The driver asked, "If you didn't request them to all be one tattoo, then how'd you get them to blend that way?"

Are we really having this conversation? I thought.

I said, "Luck, I guess."

They said nothing to that.

The driver said, "Listen here. Those waters are bad and about to get worse when it rains."

I nodded.

"You stay out of the water. You wanna swim? Go home and come back tomorrow."

I nodded again.

The passenger stepped closer and looked behind me. Looked along the sand. Then he asked, "Where's your stuff?"

"What stuff?"

"Where's your belongings?"

Which was a good question. Most of the time, I would've answered it with I don't have any stuff. But this time, I had stuff. I had a pair of navy blue track pants, which reminded me of PTUs or Physical Training Uniforms, even though they weren't shorts. And I had a tank top and a pair of flip-flops. I also had my passport, bank card, and a toothbrush. Carrying a toothbrush was the only lesson that I had learned from my father, although I never even met him. He was supposedly a drifter and former Army officer.

I said, "I don't know."

"Someone took them?"

"I don't know," I said again.

The driver asked, "If your belongings are missing, then you need to report them stolen."

These guys were very serious about their job. I thought of a smart remark to make, but I stayed quiet.

I looked around.

"Maybe you misplaced them?"

"Maybe you forgot where you put them?"

I didn't answer.

The beach was completely empty except for the three of us. In fact, the road was empty except for the occasional car passing by. In South Florida, bad weather chased everyone indoors.

I combed over the sands, thinking maybe I misplaced them. I had rolled them up in a towel that I also bought from the surf shop across the street.

I didn't see my belongings, but I did finally see the surf-board. It washed in just as I was looking north. It came in with a massive wave. The wave pushed it a few feet away from the edge of the next wave.

At least I could get back my two hundred bucks, which was good because I might not get back my bank card.

The driver followed my gaze and noticed my surfboard.

He said, "Danny, look."

The passenger looked at where he was pointing.

Danny asked, "Is that a surfer's?"

Which was a dumb question, but again I wanted to stay on their good side, so I said nothing about it.

The driver asked, "You see anyone else out there while you were swimming?"

"No. Just me."

They looked at me. Both wore the same suspicious expression, which made me realize maybe they suspected I was lying. I also thought that maybe they would concoct a farce about me drowning a swimmer and trying to steal his surfboard.

I said, "It doesn't belong to another surfer. That's my board. I was out on it. Got towed under is all. And the board got shaken loose."

"Nothing more to it, huh?"

"Nothing more to it," I said.

"How come you didn't have your leg string attached?" Danny asked.

"Leg rope."

"What?"

"It's not a leg string. It's called a leg rope."

The driver asked, "Why didn't you have yours attached?"

"I just didn't."

"That's a law here too."

I asked, "Is it?"

"Like a seatbelt law. You gotta have your leg rope attached, or you're surfing recklessly."

"I don't think so."

They both paused a beat, and the driver said, "It could be."

"It's not."

"Probably not. But it could be."

Can't be both, I thought. Then I said, "Sorry for troubling you, officers. But I'm safe, and you both helped me find my board. So, I better get it and get out of this weather."

"Hold up," Danny said. "What about your clothes?"

"There probably around here somewhere. They're probably buried in some sand or something. No big deal. I'll find them."

The driver asked, "What about your cellphone?"

"I don't have one."

They said nothing to that.

Danny said, "Hop in the truck with us. We'll drive you to pick up the board."

"I'm okay to walk. That's not far."

"What he means is get into the truck, and we'll drive you to get your board. And then we'll take you back to your car."

"Don't have a car."

They looked at each other. Then back at me.

The driver asked, "You got a hotel room here?"

I shook my head.

"Where are you living?"

I said, "I'm living right here."

"You living on the beach?"

"No. I'm living here. In my body. Same as you."

They looked at me, and then it switched to a deep stare that I believed doubled their previous suspicion.

I said, "I don't have a hotel room. I'm not sleeping anywhere that I have planned for."

"We aren't leaving you on the beach."

"Why not?"

"It's closed."

I stayed quiet.

"We done told you. The beach is closed. Now get in, and we'll pick up your board."

I shrugged.

There was no point in arguing with them. They wouldn't let me out of their sight until I was away from the beach.

So, I nodded and walked to the truck and looked in. It was

a single bench, which made me kind of glad and kind of annoyed.

Glad because no backseat or rear prisoner compartment meant they weren't meant to take prisoners, which meant they probably didn't have handcuffs. Not that I should have been worrying about handcuffs. I had done nothing wrong. At least nothing that was worthy of handcuffs.

It annoyed me because that meant I was sitting in the middle, and this was a stick shift.

I frowned as I climbed into the truck and scooted over to the middle. It was as uncomfortable as I had thought.

I am six-four and lean, but I have long legs. My knees were on the dash. I could've turned the radio knobs with my knees if the radio had knobs.

Danny and the other beach cop climbed in and shut their doors.

We backed up and drove over to the surfboard. I leaned over Danny and then back over the driver to see if I could locate my stuff.

It was a very uncomfortable, short ride.

3

THE BEACH COPS hopped out of the truck, and I got out after Danny.

I walked over to the surfboard while they watched. I picked it up and raked off some seaweed that was tangled over the fins. Then I brushed the wet sand off of it.

I looked back at the beach cops, and I said, "Looks brand new."

They nodded, not at the same time.

The driver said, "Come on, we'll drive you."

I paused a beat and asked, "Drive me where?"

"Where're you going?"

"I'm not sure."

The driver looked at Danny. Then he stepped away from the driver's side door and said, "You ain't got no clothes. No stuff. No cellphone. No hotel. Where the hell were you going to go when you left here?"

"I'll go wherever I want."

"Are you homeless?"

I paused a beat because I didn't want to answer that. So, I didn't.

One of them repeated, "Are you homeless?"

"I heard you."

"Answer me then."

"Look, fellas. I'm just a guy trying to enjoy some surfing at the beach. I don't want any trouble. Okay?"

They didn't answer.

I said, "I'm going to take my board and be on my way."

"Sir, now we have tried to be polite to you."

I nodded, but didn't agree. Polite was a strong word. More like they were overstepping their bounds with me.

"Look at yourself, sir."

"What's wrong with the way I look?"

Danny said, "You're wearing speedos."

I looked down. I wasn't wearing speedos. Speedos is actually a name brand. But in America, the brand is almost always associated with the small, brief-shaped men's swimming shorts.

"So?"

"So, we're all opened-minded here, but we don't want a homeless man walking around looking like you do in speedos. On the beach, it's okay, but not around town."

"What's wrong with the way I look?"

"Sir, please just get the board, and we'll take you to a shopping mall. You can buy some clothes."

I said, "My money is in my clothes."

"Sir, please don't make this harder than it needs to be."

I ignored them and inspected the board like I was trying to think of something else to say.

It looked all in one piece. A little water-spotted, but normal for the rough waves I put it through.

I folded it back under my arm and said, "You can't make me go, and you know it."

"Sir, don't make us slap handcuffs on you."

"Do beach cops even carry handcuffs?"

They both looked at each other.

The driver said, "We got zip ties."

He paused a beat and locked stares with me like he was waiting for me to comment. Then he said, "Danny, get the zip ties."

"Come on. You don't mean that."

"The hell I don't. You're refusing an officer of the law. We're within our rights to detain you."

For the first time, I checked out his nametag, which was a cheap-looking black rectangle thing with white font on it. His name was Ghody, which wasn't a name I remember seeing before.

I guessed it pronounced like "Cody" but with a "G."

I said, "Ghody. You know you can't detain me for doing nothing wrong."

"Ignoring 'beach closed' signs."

Danny said, "Plus, indecent exposure. Sort of."

I looked at the other one and said, "This is a public beach. I'm wearing the proper attire. Besides, unless you've got crazy laws here, a man has every right to walk around in his underwear outside. That doesn't qualify as nudity."

They said nothing to that.

I knew the zip tie thing was a bluff, anyway. If it had been a real threat, Ghody would've brandished his gun.

I said, "Fellas, you can't detain me for being on the beach when it's closed. Especially not on the sand. Not if I'm willing to leave on my own accord. You know that."

They said nothing.

"How about letting me look for my clothes? Then I'll be on my way."

Ghody said, "How'd you get that surfboard here?"

"I rented it."

"That one of Jay's?"

"I got no idea."

"The name of the shop is Jay's Surf and Stuff."

I shrugged.

Danny asked, "What's that mean?"

Ghody said, "If he's rented it from Jay's, then he paid with a bank card. Jay don't take cash for a rental."

Ghody looked at Danny, who looked dumbfounded. I can't say that I didn't get what Ghody was driving at either.

Ghody said, "It means that he's not a hobo. Hoboes don't have debit cards, Danny."

Danny nodded.

"Means he's telling the truth. I'm sorry for the confusion, mister."

Ghody seemed to relax. Honestly, I wasn't sure how to take it. I thought they were trying to rile me up for kicks. Or they really were just overdramatic. At that point, neither would've surprised me.

Just then, we heard the crackle of a police radio from the interior of the truck.

Ghody turned and nodded at Danny. I couldn't read minds, but two cops who have been partners for a while could come about as close as possible as anyone could to reading each other's minds.

My guess was that with a look, Ghody had told Danny to stay with me.

Ghody dipped his head back into the truck and responded to the dispatcher.

I couldn't hear the entire conversation. But there was an exchange of code numbers and back-and-forth radio talk.

The only thing that I could make out was a reported sighting of a man with a gun somewhere further on.

Finally, Ghody came back out and said, "Mister, good luck

finding your clothes. If you don't locate them, tell Jay to call us when you return that board."

I nodded and thanked them.

They hopped back into the truck and backed up and trailed off. They were careful not to kick up sand until they got farther away, and then they sped off.

I watched them without budging until they turned a corner on the main drive and were lost to sight.

4

I FOUND my pants and my flip-flops about where I had left them. The reason that I hadn't seen them before was that they hadn't been there before.

I carried the surfboard back about fifty yards. Just in time to see my pants wash into the edge of the Atlantic Ocean.

I frowned.

I bent down and bundled them up, one-handed. I held them out by the waistband and let the legs ripple down and untangle themselves.

They were soaked.

I dropped the surfboard a yard away in the damp sand, and then I sieved through the pockets until I found my belongings. Everything was still there, but soaked. The bank card would still work, and I could wash off the toothbrush, but I wondered if there would be any problems with the passport getting wet.

The toothbrush wouldn't fold like it was meant to. It was jammed sticking out straight. I left it.

I wrung the pants out as best I could, and then I whipped them twice to dry them.

I slipped them back on. They weren't much drier than I had been anyway, since my towel was also missing.

I stood up tall and looked left and looked right. I scanned the shore and then the incoming surf.

I saw nothing—no sign of my t-shirt or my towel. I guess none of that was a big deal, since I had just bought it all this morning in the surf shop.

I would've rented the towel, but the owner, Jay I presumed, had outsmarted me and only had towels for sale.

I paid full sticker price. I was almost more upset that my towel had gotten washed out to sea over the rest of my missing clothes. I got little use out of it, and I paid full price for it.

I walked along the shoreline, going south because it was the direction away from Jay's Surf Shop. I figured I would walk for a bit and see what I found.

If I found nothing, then I would turn back after several minutes and double back, giving myself two chances to search the beach.

I only made it five minutes because I stepped on something metal.

It jabbed my big toe on my right foot. It didn't stab me because it wasn't sharp-edged.

I bent down and saw a thin-sided metal object poking out of the sand. It looked like it was buried a little deep, but the heavy waves and outgoing tide had unearthed it.

I reached down and pinched two fingers around it and dragged it.

I knew it was a necklace because it had a long chain of small metal beads. I picked it up quickly and a second later; I knew it was more than a necklace.

I held it out in front of my face.

It dangled and twisted and spun in the wind.

I was looking at a pair of dog tags.

I brushed off the wet sand so that I could read the information. Something was very, very wrong about these dog tags.

All the normal information was there, plain as day. There was a social security number. There was a religious preference. And there was a blood type.

But there was no name.

Where a last and first name were supposed to be, there was nothing but scratch marks and holes dug through the metal.

5

SOMEONE WENT to a lot of trouble and time and elbow grease just to erase the name off the dog tags.

My guess was that someone had filed the name off with half a jagged edge and half a sharp edge. And they had done it with a lot of care. The scratch patterns traced the same trail left by the previous action, one after the next. It was like looking and judging the difference between a lawn cut by a professional lawn man and a lawn cut by a four-year-old who couldn't reach the pedals of a tractor.

The patterns were straight and side by side and flawless, which made me think this guy had done this before.

My best bet was it was someone who had a lot of practice filing metal.

Filing off things usually incorporated filing off numbers such as serial numbers. And filing off serial numbers was usually something that went against the intent of the manufacturer. And it was usually illegal, such as the serial numbers on a gun.

Whoever the guy was, he took his time to scratch off his name.

Yet there was something violent about the way he did it. Something final. Something absolute.

I couldn't quite put my finger on it. Not specifically. But I knew the energy and the planning that was put into it. I understood that part.

It was done with respect and with great effort and care. But there appeared to be something angry behind it.

Maybe the owner wanted to erase his own name from the registry of the military. Maybe he wanted nothing else to do with it. Like he had rejected that part of his life. But he couldn't just scratch through the name haphazardly, out of a sense of respect.

Then again, he also threw his dog tags into the ocean, which was a gesture of contempt for the military.

US military-issued dog tags were all the same. And yet they were all different in small ways.

Each branch of the US forces had its own diminutive peccadilloes about where information was placed and what information was required and what information was allowed.

The Air Force followed the social security number with an "AF" to show the branch of service.

The Marines had their social security number in a three/two/four format. They separated the groupings of numbers with spaces: no comma, no dash, no period—just spaces.

On a separate line, following the social security number, they also showed the branch of the user's station with a *USMC*, which stood for: *United States Marine Corps*.

But they also went a step further. They showed the wearer's gasmask size, which was stamped in an "S" for small, an "M" for medium, and an "L" for large.

I wondered who the hell wore large? Unless the large was the American large, which was mainly a popular size in clothing because it meant more room. And like most Americans, I liked more room in my clothes.

Thinking about this made me smile because I was wearing speedos, which were not famous for room-giving priorities.

I guess I prefer snug underwear. Everything else, I prefer plenty of legroom.

Then there were the Army and the Coast Guard and the Navy.

Of course, I knew the Navy, and I knew the Navy's dog tags. These weren't Navy.

I was sure that the dog tags were Army. They used last name, first and middle initial. Then they posted social security number and blood type and religion.

I wasn't Army. I had never been Army. The last time I heard about Army dog tags, they were considering moving away from using a soldier's social security number. I guess because it gave out private information. That was a grave concern to many people. With everything being internet-based nowadays, identity theft was a real issue.

Of course, getting a look at a soldier's dog tags without his or her knowledge was very difficult. But possible. I imagine a scorned lover might memorize them when the user was in the shower. Easy enough.

What was amazing to me was that the green machine was the first to make this change, losing the social security number. I would've thought that it would've been the Air Force, for sure.

The Air Force was the most liberal out of the uniformed services. Nothing wrong with that. We had a joke in the Navy. We called them the Chair Force, which was a jab out of love, naturally.

Chair Forcers did the best with change. Certainly not the Army. The Army hated change.

After a second look at the social security number, I realized it was not the social security number.

A social security number has nine digits the last time I checked.

This number had ten.

It was the Department of Defense Identification Number assigned to members of the armed forces.

The Army must've made the switch after all.

The only thing that I was unsure of was whether that meant that they reissued everyone a new dog tag after they made the switch. Or did they only give out the updated dog tags to new recruits after this policy was started?

I had no idea.

But if the answer was the latter, that meant that the wearer's tags were recent.

I stood up and tucked the dog tags into my front pocket.

It was something that I would have to think about later because the rain started. It was nothing, but it would turn into something soon.

I heard a thunderclap—loud and booming in the distance.

More lightning *cracked*, and I saw the flash over the water. The flicker echoed and bounced off the underbelly of the storm clouds.

I scooped up the rented surfboard and headed back to the surf shop to return the board.

6

I GOT BACK my two hundred bucks. The kid behind the counter said it would go back onto my card.

I thanked him and asked about the local army bases.

He said that there were several Army Reserve Stations in the region.

The closest wasn't an Army base or a reserve station. It was a Florida National Guard base, but I wanted an Army base. The kid said there was one farther north.

After I left the surf shop, I waited out under a canopy at the entrance and watched the rain turn from a steady drizzle into a hard thrashing.

I sat on a bench next to a covered wastebasket with a plastic ashtray insert on top. The tray was full of ashes. I was surprised to see it. Surfers and people around Cocoa Beach struck me as the healthy type. I had seen no one smoking since I got there. And I had been in town for about a week. It was the start of summer, and I liked the beach. Where else would I be?

This area was a big surfing community. Some of the most famous American surfers in the world took refuge here.

I had seen plenty of surfers smoking on the beach at night, but they were smoking cigarettes rolled with something other than pure tobacco that I knew for sure.

There's a big difference in smell between traditional tobacco and marijuana.

I had been around enough sailors and Navy ships to know the smell of both.

I didn't smoke either, but I only had prejudices against the former. Everyone knew for a fact that modern cigarettes caused cancer. No one had any evidence that marijuana caused anything but laziness.

Still, my drug of choice was the caffeinated Colombian kind.

The rain continued to fall.

I stayed out in front of the shop under the canopy until I got both cold and impatient.

I went back to the shop and buy some new clothes. I kept the pants because they were getting closer to dry by this point. I guessed that technically they were damp, but I had grown oddly comfortable in them.

I bought a long-sleeved surfer shirt. It was white with a logo of a surfer brand I wasn't familiar with. That didn't mean that it was not a popular brand. I just was never much up on fashion.

Of course, I had heard of the old brands like Polo or Ralph Lauren or Calvin Klein. But I didn't know which brands were in style and which were not. I had zero idea what the current trends were in almost anything—especially fashion.

I also bought a black hooded windbreaker made of nylon and claiming to be water-resistant on the tag. It was expensive, but then again, I was at the mercy of the shop and the local prices.

Cocoa Beach wasn't the kind of town to go price comparing in. Almost everyone who shopped on the beach was going to be a tourist. And even the locals were used to paying high prices.

I imagined that most of South Florida was the same.

I hadn't been to Miami in nearly a decade. Or at least the last time that I remember being there had been that long ago. Recently, I stopped there. South Beach had changed little. But other parts of the city had been built up dramatically.

Ten years ago, the downtown part was cheap and drab. Now it was all built up. There were dozens of high rises. Back then, the downtown part was overrun with slum buildings and the homeless. Now it was overrun with overpriced condos and international banks.

I also grabbed a pair of tennis shoes. Like the windbreaker, they weren't cheap, but they were the cheapest pair that had my shoe size.

I tossed the flip-flops into the trashcan, which made the store clerk look at me cockeyed. But he said nothing about it. I went back outside under the canopy and sat on the bench. I slipped the shoes on. No socks. And I took out the shirt and the windbreaker and stuffed the store's bag into the wastebasket with the ashtray.

I put everything on and zipped up the windbreaker. I pulled the hood up over my head and walked north.

I headed north because it was to my left and also because of my mother. Way back when I was a little kid, she had taught me always to look left and then right before crossing the street. And left had been the first direction I looked when I stepped out of the surf shop parking lot.

I was not trying to walk to the nearest Army Reserve Station. I was looking for coffee.

I found a diner chain that was serving breakfast. This location looked old and in need of renovations, but the coffee was good, and the place was clean.

The coffee was good and black and caffeinated.

Since the rain looked like it wouldn't let up soon, I ordered two eggs, scrambled, and toast and bacon.

It all came out twenty minutes later, which was a long wait, but I didn't complain because I never saw the bottom of my mug. The waitress was on top of her game.

She was a real pro.

I ate everything on my plate and paid the check and tipped the waitress a dollar extra. Which seemed to confuse her, like maybe the rest of her customers tipped her less because of the slow food delivery times.

Before I left, she gave me directions to the nearest Army Reserve Station, which was within driving distance.

She must've known that I was from out of town because she suggested that I Uber there.

I knew what Uber was. And it sounded like a great service, but I didn't have a cellphone, and therefore I didn't have the app required to request an Uber.

I hated taxis. I always had.

All over the world, taking a taxi was a fifty-fifty prospect for prices and customer service. The thing about Uber that I had heard people brag about was that the service was always top-notch, and the prices were low or at least competitive when compared to taxi rides.

After she told me about Uber, I asked her if there was a bus station nearby. She pointed me toward a local bus stop.

Most military installations are usually built somewhere near a bus route. And often, military bases were stops on bus routes.

Most of the United States' military personnel started out in the low-income bracket. Many new recruits didn't have personal vehicles. Therefore, they used buses.

I thanked her and left and walked to the bus stop.

I was headed to an Army Reserve Station called Graham.

7

GRAHAM WAS ABOUT twenty klicks north of the bus stop, which led me to change buses twice. The last one was one of those old trolleys.

A guy in the seat next to me had called it a "Beach Comber" while he was trying to explain to me how he had to go out of his way every day to catch it in order to get to work as a custodian at a local elementary school because his car was in the shop every other month.

According to him, the "Beach Comber" was more of a pain in the ass than his car because half the time, it was late.

He seemed happy that this hadn't been one of those occasions.

The guy asked me what my line of work was, but I didn't have to answer since we were at my stop.

I told him to take it easy, and I disembarked.

By that point, the rain had slowed and died down to a borderline drizzle.

Graham wasn't much of an installation.

I was familiar with Army installations as much as I had

been with sites for any other branch of the military that I hadn't been in.

I had seen other branches' installations and bases. And I had passed through many of them for various reasons and various coordination procedures in co-managed operations.

It had a fence and a gate and a guard hut. There were low buildings. All green. All without character or taste or anything unique to them.

The Army always took the uniform idea all the way.

They would have their soldiers all think the same thoughts if they could.

I couldn't tell how many acres made up the base, but it was a lot. It wasn't enough to qualify it as a major base, and it was far from looking important. But it wasn't a small installation either. I had seen much smaller. This one probably had a base commander who was ranked higher than colonel, but far from a one-star.

I could see that beyond the guard hut, there was a moderate amount of street and foot traffic. Men and women in uniform walking and talking. Some were going here. Others went there.

Some carried briefcases. Others carried papers.

Some of them looked hurried, and others looked casual.

It was all habitual military work.

The rain stopped, but the dark clouds hung around like they had no place else to go.

I approached the base.

The guard behind the traffic barriers saw me coming. He called back to the guard hut, and two more soldiers stepped out of the hut and walked down to the tip of the station. They stopped and stood in a practiced guard stance. I had seen similar ones before, and I had probably seen this positioning before. But I had no idea what it was called.

It was an army thing, not a Navy or Marine thing. They had their own training and their own strategies. But like all corporations, nothing was unique with tactics.

Live long enough, and you'll come across the same bullshit that you've seen before.

A gravy-colored Buick was waiting to clear the hut and drive onto the base. One guard remained with it, while the other two stepped away from the station and approached me.

I figured they were waiting to see my intent before confronting me.

I might have been just passing around the base, which made no sense to me because it looked like the road around the base led to nothing but trees.

They stopped well ahead of me, as if they knew the borders of their jurisdiction, and that was the edge.

I walked closer and stopped.

They all wore the same woodland pattern camos. They wore black flak vests with multiple Velcro pockets and inserts, stuffed with flashlights and road flares and extendable batons. They probably had extra bullets hidden away in there somewhere.

They wore black berets with insignias patched on the front.

Holstered on their right sides were Beretta M9s, the standard pistol for the Army Military Police Corps.

One MP was a woman. She was shorter than the other two. But she looked like she packed quite the punch.

The male MP had walked out in front of her and stopped at the crescent of a patch of grass, just beyond the curb, which put him about four inches shorter than me.

He said, "Sir, can I help you?"

Casually, I looked him up and down. He had the military police patch south of his left shoulder, just above his bicep.

Above that was an armband that had the abbreviation: *MP* sewn on.

His nametape read: *Hamilton*. Like the president.

I said, "I need to speak to your CO."

"Who are you?"

I didn't want to diddle-daddle around with a long back-and-forth pissing contest. So, I used the old double-dealing trick of flattery.

I said, "Captain Hamilton, my name is Jack Widow. I have a matter to discuss with your CO. It's not an emergency or anything. Nothing to get all riled up about. I simply want to report a possible crime."

Hamilton cocked his head and said, "Mr. Widow, I appreciate the promotion, but I'm not a captain. I'm a second lieutenant."

He veered off for a brief pause and looked past me like he was going to say that he wished he were a captain. And then I sensed maybe he was supposed to have been one already. Like it had been in his plans for himself, but not in the cards for him.

A hint of envy sparkled in his eyes.

Then he said, "What crime do you want to report?"

"I didn't say it was a crime. I said 'possible' crime. Like maybe. Like I'm not sure what it is."

"Any threat of a crime is taken seriously here, sir."

I stayed quiet.

Hamilton said, "Are you here to threaten a crime? On military property?"

"I said I want to report something. I didn't threaten a crime."

Hamilton paused, looked me up and down like he was showing me he was assessing me.

I said, "You guys guard this base like you've got something important here to protect."

"Sir, we're MPs in the United States Army. We are doing our duty."

"Relax, Lieutenant. I'm familiar with military cops."

"Are you a disgruntled former soldier?"

I didn't answer that. Instead, I said, "Lieutenant, are you going to show me to your chief or not?"

He paused another brief second, and then he said, "We don't have a chief here."

"You got a station commander?"

"We do."

"Then, he'll do just fine."

Hamilton stayed still and looked at me again, like he was deciding whether to bother the station commander or to shoot me in the kneecaps and then introduce me to the station commander.

I noticed his BDUs were a little sun-bleached, like he had just gotten back from a deployment in the desert. Then again, the sun will do that in South Florida too.

He said, "Stay here, please, sir."

I didn't have to speak to his CO to report the dog tags, but I didn't know the circumstances of them.

Graham was the nearest Army installation to town, and I had figured that there was just as much chance that the tags were stolen or lost, and that someone other than the wearer could've vandalized them.

If the owner had lost them, that could be embarrassing. If he had mutilated them himself, then that could be a criminal offense. Either way, I thought it safer to keep the bubble of people who knew about it small.

Hamilton stepped back and away from the crescent and left the female MP to watch me.

I watched him pass the other guard, and he stopped and whispered to him.

The other guard finished inspecting the car that was attempting entry and waived the driver in. Then he nodded to the lieutenant and walked over to join me and the female MP.

They were my guards, standing post and keeping me out of trouble.

I stayed standing and looked over the base. Again, I saw nothing particularly special about it, nothing that was cause for such an uproar over a civilian standing at the gate. I understood times were different ever since 9/11.

Military bases and military police all over the world were far more high-strung than they had been in previous years. It used to be suicide bombers, were a thing of fiction. And then they were a real occurrence, but it only happened "over there."

Now, everything was different, and it wasn't going back to what it was in the old days.

So far, there had never been a suicide bombing on US soil related to today's Islamic terrorists that resulted in innocent deaths. The only thing close was a suicide bombing at a university in Oklahoma back in 2005. The only person killed in that one was the bomber himself.

I said, "You guys take your job here pretty seriously?"

"Sir?" the female MP asked.

The male said, "Keep quiet, Maxine."

I looked at him for a sign of rank, but the Army MP BDU doesn't show rank. So, I had no idea if he outranked her or not.

I settled on looking at his nametape. His name was Coresca. I glanced left over at her nametape. The nametape on the female MP read: *Maxine*.

It wasn't her first name. It was her last. I had never heard Maxine as a last name before. But then again, I had never heard of Coresca either.

I said, "Do you outrank her, soldier?"

Coresca looked at me and said, "Sir, it's not your business to know military affairs."

"Wrong."

"What's that?"

"You're wrong, Coresca?"

"How's that, sir?"

"I'm a civilian. I'm a taxpayer. Therefore, my taxes built this base. They maintain this base. Your uniform was bought with taxpayer money. Your cot was bought with taxpayer money."

He paused a beat, and then he said, "I don't sleep on a cot."

"Then the bed in your house was bought with taxpayer money. Whatever."

"I bought my bed with my own money."

I said, "From your government salary. Which I provided."

He said nothing.

I said, "If you think about it. Even the toilet you sit on, I bought."

Silence.

"Your ass literally belongs to the civilians of this country."

He stayed quiet.

Maxine smirked and let out a giggle.

Coresca shot her a quick glance. And she suppressed her giggle, said nothing.

I said, "So your business actually is my business."

He switched gears and said, "Sir, are you being hostile to a United States military officer?"

"Are you an officer?" I asked.

"Sir, yes, I'm an officer."

"You seem more like a grunt to me."

"Sir, now you're being openly hostile to a United States Military Policeman on Army property."

"Calm down, Private. I'm just talking. I made no open threats to you."

Just then, Coresca looked like he wanted to say something more. But he was interrupted because Hamilton came back out of the guard hut.

He called out to me and waved me forward.

Coresca sneered at me, and I smiled at him. I made a point of passing him by without looking at him. To me, it was a friendly rivalry. Soldiers, marines, airmen, and sailors have expressed rivalry since the beginning of time.

I thought nothing more about it. And I didn't care if Coresca did or not.

Hamilton stood out in front of the front gate and waited for me to reach him.

I stopped in front and felt Coresca and Maxine walk up behind me.

He said, "You two, back to work."

Coresca moved back to tending to the cars that drove up, and Maxine moved over to the exit side.

Hamilton said, "I just got off the phone with my SC. He isn't here right now, but he said that you can report to me whatever the crime is that you have to report."

I stayed quiet.

"I'm the ranking officer right now at this station for the MPs."

I thought about it, and then I shrugged.

I said, "Sure."

"You want to do it somewhere else?"

"I think it might be something that is better kept quiet."

"Okay. You got a name?"

"Jack Widow."

"Mr. Widow, can I see your identification?"

I reached into my back pocket and pulled out my passport. It was still damp from the rain and the Atlantic Ocean.

I may have to get a new one, I thought.

I handed it to him. He took it and kept it out for me to see, and walked back into the guard hut. He dumped himself down onto a high-back stool and swiveled around to face a computer.

He hit the keyboard and started accessing a program to print a temporary visitor badge for me; I assumed.

Hamilton opened my passport. He made no comment about it being damp. Instead, he stopped and stared at the pages of the many, many foreign stamps that I had in it.

He looked up at me and said, "You sure travel a lot, Mr. Widow."

I nodded.

Then he looked at the stamps. He stopped on one and asked, "What were you doing in Iran?"

Usually, I would've responded with a "none of your business," but I didn't see any reason to lie to start anything here with the guy. So, I said, "I was in the Navy. We used to do business with a lot of foreign countries. Sometimes I had to go to all sorts of places."

That was about as much truth that I wanted to reveal.

One of the major functions of the Navy was counterintelligence. He would know that.

He would also know that to be effective in counterintelligence; we had to engage with unsavory people. Many of our contacts were in the foreign jurisdictions of countries that America wasn't on the best of terms with. This certainly included Iran.

He nodded, and then he said, "You must've been pretty

important in the Navy to be trusted with missions that took you into enemy territory."

I shrugged and said, "I was just a regular guy."

"What were you, black ops? SOG?"

SOG was the CIA's Special Operations Group, which was about as vague a name as anything else. And it was all because of the word "Group." What group?

It just meant that it was whatever group the CIA incorporated into the fold.

They often recruited from the SEALs for their special operators.

"The SEALs."

He sat straight on the stool and stared at me.

He asked, "What team?"

"I can't tell you that much."

"Are you still active?"

"No."

He nodded and took the passport and stuck it underneath some kind of scanner. A light flashed and scanned the passport, but nothing popped up on his computer screen. He tried again. Same thing. I guessed that the saltwater bath had destroyed the electronic chip.

Hamilton keyed in the number, and my face came up.

He hit a few keys and used a wireless mouse to click yes and 'no' on a couple of boxes.

A moment later, he was slipping a plastic badge with my face on it into a plastic case.

He handed it to me and said, "Clip that on your shirt."

I took it and looked at it. I saw my passport photo and some pedigree information that was duplicated from my passport and the word: "VISITOR," printed in all caps and in bold red font.

I pinched a metal clasp on the case and clipped it to the

bottom of my T-shirt neckband. It hung on the top of my chest, inside the open windbreaker.

Hamilton said, "Keep that visible."

I nodded.

"Follow me."

Hamilton stood up and led me through the front gate. We walked two blocks north and took a right at a four-way intersection.

"Here. Let's go in here."

He led the way into an unmarked office building and through a set of double doors.

The Army was all about the bare minimum for their buildings. The walls, the doors, the tiles on the floor, the tiles on the ceiling, and even the paint was all the same. Not the same colors, but they all had the same standardization to them, like every nook and cranny in the Army's design for the base was all taken from the same page of the same catalog for military design.

Nothing ever changes in the Army.

I wasn't sure what kind of office building this was. There were soldiers—men and women—standing around, sitting at cubicles, sitting at small round tables, conversing about Army business.

Everyone stopped and stared at me as I passed them by. Then they returned to whatever they had been doing before.

I followed Hamilton into a back office that was empty. There was a desk at the center of the room and a small steel desk fan on the corner. It was on and blowing and rotating. A thin string blew out from the mesh grill as it rotated from one point and back to the next.

Hamilton didn't sit at the desk. Instead, he led us over to a small round table in the corner behind the door and said, "Have a seat, Widow."

I pulled out the chair and sat down.

He said, "Want coffee or a coke or something?"

"I appreciate the hospitality, but I don't think I'll be here long enough for that."

"We'll be here a few minutes, Widow."

"What I have to report may not be that big a deal."

"You had me call my boss. So now we're going to sit here and go through the motions."

I said, "Can I get a coffee, then?"

"Yes. Stay here a minute."

I nodded and stayed sitting.

Hamilton went to the door, stepped out. I heard him call out to someone and ask him to bring us some coffee. Then he peeked his head back into the room and asked, "You take sugar?"

"Black is fine."

He nodded and left again.

Hamilton came back into the room and stayed. He had a clipboard in his hand, but I had no idea where it came from. I didn't see him pick it up.

He laid my passport out and open on the tabletop. He kept his left-hand middle finger in the book's corner to prop it open and as close to flat as it would get.

I watched him pull a ballpoint pen out of his shirt pocket. He clicked the top and wrote on the first page of a document that was stapled to at least one other page on the clipboard.

He didn't look up. He didn't speak for a good minute. He just wrote and filled out information from my passport.

I assumed it was: name, place of birth, and so on.

Another minute went by, and there was a single knock at the door.

Hamilton said, "Come in."

A young black soldier walked in. He nodded at me first, and then he said, "I've got your coffee, Lieutenant."

"Come in. Come in."

The soldier shuffled in with two plain white mugs. He held them, one-handed. His thumb and index finger slipped through the handles of both. He used his free hand to push the door open, and he squeezed in through it.

He set the mugs down first and stood straight and pulled a few packets of white sugar out of his pants pocket and dropped them on the table near the coffee.

He said, "Anything else for you, sir?"

"That's all, Jarson."

The soldier named Jarson smiled and stood straight and saluted Hamilton. Which gave me the impression that it was done only because I was there. Hamilton seemed a little slack with his guys compared to other COs that I had known.

I said nothing about it.

Hamilton said, "Take your pick."

I reached forward and took a coffee. I stared into the cup like I could inspect it on sight alone. That wasn't a possibility, not for me, but I could smell it. And this smelled like the real deal. A fresh aroma. Newly brewed.

I took a slow sip, partly to test its heat and partly to test its flavor. It was pretty good. The soldier named Jarson knew his craft well.

I said, "You should promote him."

Hamilton looked up from the clipboard and asked, "What?"

"Jarson, you should promote him. This is a hell of a cup of coffee."

"I prefer mine with sugar," he said, and he set the pen down and tore open four packets of sugar and let them landslide down into his coffee.

I said nothing about it.

Hamilton retrieved his pen, and then he slid my passport back over to me.

He asked, "Okay, Mr. Widow. What crime do you wish to report?"

I reached into my pocket and pulled out the dog tags.

I said, "I found these on Cocoa Beach."

He cocked his head and reached over and took the dog tags from me. He stared at them, noticed the same thing that I had noticed, the scratched-off name.

He held them up in the air and let the ball chain spin and tangle.

He said, "That is peculiar."

8

"Why do you suppose the name is scratched off?" Hamilton asked.

"I've got no idea."

"Looks like it wasn't done hastily either. There's a symmetry to it."

I nodded.

He continued to study it for longer, and then he looked at me. He said, "Mr. Widow. I see now why the secrecy. If someone ditched his dog tags and scratched his own name off, then this could be a crime. But if someone stole it and did this then, it could be embarrassing. Especially if this was an officer."

Especially if it was done by a lover scorned, I thought.

I nodded.

Hamilton set the dog tags down on the tabletop and wrote some more on the document.

He did this for another couple of minutes, and we sat in silence. Then he flipped to the second page and looked at me.

He asked, "Give me your account of how you found it. Leave nothing out."

I told him my account of what had happened. But I didn't admit some of it. I left off the part about the beach cops—no reason to drag them into a lost or stolen dog tag.

Hamilton wrote it all down in a box that took up half of the second page, and then he set his pen down and said, "This is interesting. Can I ask you to hang around a bit?"

I thought about it. I thought about how this was one of the first times that a cop asked me to stick around and not ordered me to. Better take advantage of this rare occurrence.

I said, "Get me another cup of coffee, and you got a deal."

"Sure thing. Jarson will bring you one. You can wait down the hall. There's a sofa."

I nodded and stood up, took my cup. It was empty.

"I'm gonna call my SC, and I'll get back to you. Shouldn't take too long."

I shrugged and said, "My only plans are to move forward. But I can stick around for a cup of coffee."

He nodded and called Jarson in.

Jarson took me out into his little section of their department and showed me to a small sofa. He took my cup and disappeared to return with another one.

Hamilton disappeared back into his office and shut the door.

I dumped myself down on the sofa, and Jarson returned a minute later with another cup of coffee.

He said, "I'm making a new pot now."

I thanked him, but figured I wouldn't be around long enough for another cup.

I was wrong, and I was right.

I would be there a lot longer, but I wouldn't have another cup.

Coffee's too hard to drink in handcuffs.

9

THEY CAME for me with weapons drawn.

I sat on the sofa—coffee in one hand and an old paperback copy of *Atlas Shrugged*, dog-eared and open, in the other.

I found it underneath a pile of magazines on a small end table. I also found a current issue of the *Army Times*.

I wasn't interested in current events at the moment.

I page-turned through Ayn Rand's classic until Hamilton came back. I didn't have to wait long for someone to come in and let me know what was next. But it wasn't Hamilton.

Coresca entered from the hallway into the secretarial pen with two other MPs that I hadn't seen before. He burst in first with a look of satisfaction and professionalism on his face. One look outshone the other.

A polished Army issued Beretta M9 gleamed under the bright overhead LED lights. The Beretta was in his hand. The barrel pointed at the ground until he saw me. Then his arms moved fast. Quick reflexes, not faster than mine. But fast reflexes didn't matter because I wasn't the one armed.

The M9 pointed right at my center mass.

My coffee mug had been out in front of me at that moment. I was mid-attempt in taking another pull from it.

If Coresca fired the M9 my blood would've splattered out of my chest along with the black coffee.

It made me think of one of those Jackson Pollock paintings. Black and red colors sprayed across a white canvas, like the wall behind me.

I stared at the end of the gun and was a little hurt because, for once, I thought I was going to get reasonable treatment from cops.

Coresca said nothing, but he gave me a grin.

The other two MPs stepped past him and to his right and left sides.

Jarson wheeled away from his desk in his office chair. He had a genuine look of shock on his face. Which I believed was authentic.

He asked, "What's going on?"

Again, he sounded authentic. He either was surprised or he should've been in show business.

Coresca stopped dead center in the room, about five feet from me, which I was sure was written somewhere in an Army SOP manual, filed away under apprehending a suspect in a confined, indoor space.

He said, "Hold it! Jack Widow, you are under arrest!"

The other two MPs sidestepped in different directions—each of them flanking Coresca and each of them pointing similar M9s at me.

I moved slowly and reached forward, set the coffee mug onto the edge of Jarson's desk.

I could've used it as a thrown weapon, like a hot liquid Molotov cocktail, but I wasn't here to burn an Army MP for doing his job.

I raised my hands and used my abs to pull myself up off the sofa. I stood. The MPs stayed where they were.

I asked, "What the hell is this?"

"I told ya. This is an arrest."

I shook my head and said, "You can't arrest me. I'm a civilian."

"You're on Army property. Therefore, we can arrest you."

Then he acted like he waited for me to say something, but I didn't.

He spouted off some Army regulation statute that may or may not have been true. He claimed it gave him the right to arrest me.

I asked, "On what charge?"

Hamilton walked out of his office at that moment. He gave me a look that made me feel a little betrayed.

He said, "We don't have to charge you with anything. We're not the ones who want you."

I stayed quiet.

He said, "We're arresting you because the FBI wants us to."

10

CORESCA CUFFED ME.

He ratcheted the cuffs tight on my wrists, and he did it slowly. On purpose. Deliberate. Like shoulder checking a guy in a crowded hallway. Both guys know what happened, but no one else caught it.

I guessed he was waiting for me to complain about it because afterward; he stood there, silent, with a smirk on his face.

I stayed quiet. I wouldn't give him the satisfaction.

All three MPs holstered their weapons. I noticed Coresca kept his safety buckle unsnapped on his holster.

I looked at Hamilton, avoided eye contact with Coresca.

I asked, "The FBI? For what?"

Hamilton said, "It turns out, Mr. Widow, that they're quite interested in the dog tags you found."

He paused a beat, and then he said, "Allegedly, found."

"I told you. I found them down on Cocoa Beach. Give me a map, and I'll tell you exactly where."

Hamilton said, "That's not up to me, Widow. That's up to the Feds."

I ground my teeth and took a long, deep breath.

I asked, "How long is this going to take?"

"I got no idea."

Coresca asked, "Wanna put him in holding?"

Because the base was small, I was surprised to hear Coresca call any part of it "holding." I imagined that the best they would have would be a single cell, maybe two. It was doubtful that Graham would have a need for more than that.

Hamilton said, "Yes."

Coresca grabbed the cuffs from behind me and jerked them down and pointed me to a northern direction like he was steering me.

"Easy, Coresca. Mr. Widow is a civilian."

Hamilton looked at me and said, "Don't take it personally, Widow. Your story might be true, and it might not. I don't know. It's not for me to say. The FBI is sending someone, and you'll be on your way soon."

"I take it personally."

Hamilton said nothing to that.

Coresca pushed me forward, and I moved.

I said, "You don't need to push."

Coresca didn't answer, but he let go of my cuffs.

Using verbal commands, he led me where to go and stayed close behind. One of the other MPs walked out in front of me and the second one followed behind until we got to the end of one hall and then stepped through an open push door and onto the sidewalk.

One of the MPs turned and walked in the other direction, leaving me with just the two.

Part of me thought that was a mistake. Handcuffed behind my back or not, I could've figured out a way of taking out two guys. There's always a way.

But I complied and followed the first MP down the sidewalk and past two small buildings. Then we turned on a service drive and walked up a short ramp to a building with thin windows.

Inside, I was pretty shocked to find a holding cell that was more than just one cell. There were three. One large one, and two across the hall from it, were basically just the same cell, cut in half.

They were all empty, which was not surprising.

Coresca grabbed my handcuffs again and pulled them back—tight.

He said, "Stop!"

I stopped.

The other guard took out a set of keys and opened the door to one of the small cells, and stepped back. To make room for me, I supposed.

Coresca said, "Get in."

I stepped in, turned, and watched the barred door slam shut.

"Come here and turn around," Coresca said.

I didn't move. I never like turning my back on a potential threat.

"I'm just gonna take the cuffs off," he said.

Reluctantly, I moved back to the cell door, and he removed the cuffs and walked away. I twisted my wrists, happy for at least that part of my body to be free, and got ready to wait.

I was good at waiting—almost as much as I was used to getting thrown in jail.

The dog tags were key to whatever the hell was going on. That much I knew for sure. Beyond that, I knew nothing.

There was no sense in kicking up dust or complaining or making a big fuss over something that they wouldn't tell me about.

I did the only thing that I could. I slept.

The jail cell didn't have a cot or anything that would pass for a bed. But there was a long bench that was good enough. I took off the windbreaker and balled it up and used it as a pillow.

I closed my eyes and slept.

11

THE WAIT WAS SHORT.

However, I wouldn't have known that at first, because I had fallen asleep.

I was woken up by the sound of Coresca's voice. He shouted at me like a boot camp drill instructor. Which, I figured, was a bullshit attempt to intimidate me, like a gorilla beating his chest. I was in his house, his domain, and he was going to make sure that I knew it.

It didn't work.

He said, "Wake up, Widow! Your ride's here!"

I opened my eyes. Bright light rushed my face, and my eyes squinted and clenched.

The light came from the overhead lamps that lit the hall between the cells. They had been on the entire time, but I had tuned them out and forgotten about them.

Before I dozed off, I had instinctively flung my arm across my face, blocking out the light.

I sat up, groggy, and, honestly, disoriented. I felt like I had been drugged. I must've been extremely tired and not realized it.

"Come on! Get up, Widow! Sleep time's over!"

I yawned and stretched and stood up. Then I stretched some more. I must admit I did a little of it on purpose. Nothing pisses off guys like Coresca more than making them feel insignificant. Having a prisoner who doesn't listen to commands, who isn't fazed by his tactics of intimidation, only makes guys like Coresca feel inadequate.

I smiled.

He said, "Widow! Step to the door, already! Time to go!"

Lethargically and sluggishly, I followed his instructions and stepped to the door.

Coresca was alone this time. No one came with him. No backup. No one to help him in case I decided I wanted out. I guess he thought he could handle me alone.

I noticed that his safety button on his holster was unsnapped again.

I said, "You really should snap that button closed. I'm sure Army regulation requires armed soldiers to have it snapped at all times."

I paused a second, and then I said, "Especially Army MPs. Unless you face a clear and present danger."

Coresca didn't respond. He didn't look down at his gun holster like he had forgotten about it being unsnapped, which was what a normal person, who had forgotten, would've done.

A normal person would've glanced at it, realized the mistake, and felt embarrassed that a prisoner had noticed that he made a grave violation of military regulation. But Coresca didn't do that.

He didn't do that because he knew it was unsnapped. He had it unsnapped on purpose.

"Why is it unsnapped? Do you see me as a clear and present danger?"

He said nothing.

I asked, "You planning to shoot me with that gun?"

"Don't give me a reason, Widow!"

I stayed quiet.

"Step out!"

Coresca opened the barred door with the keys in one hand and the other hand near his gun, but not touching it.

I smiled and stepped forward, keeping my palms out and obvious. I didn't want to get shot because he had a superficial problem with me. I didn't want him to have a shred of probable cause for drawing his gun.

The guy had itchy trigger finger written on his forehead.

Coresca said, "Face the bars."

I turned and faced the bars. I put my hands behind my back. I knew he was going to cuff me again. I didn't need to wait for him to tell me.

He slapped the cuffs on me and tightened them, just like before.

The hand that was not near his gun gripped under my bicep and pulled me away from the bars, and then pushed me out in front of him.

"Walk," he said.

I smiled and complied.

We walked out of the building and back down the service ramp and onto the sidewalk. We passed the same two buildings as before, but this time we passed the building that I had been sitting in with Hamilton.

We walked back to the gate.

I saw the same female MP from before and a new MP, who was stopping incoming cars, taking their licenses and letting them pass.

Hamilton stood inside the gate, waiting for me.

Beyond him, outside the gate, I saw the back of a black SUV, unmarked. It looked like it had pulled into the gate and made a U-turn so that it could face the other direction.

The brake lights gleamed, and car exhaust pooled underneath the tailpipe. Someone was seated in it with the engine running.

My escort, I presumed.

Hamilton said, "Follow me."

I followed behind him. Coresca wasn't far behind me. He was so close that I could feel the vibrations from his boots on the blacktop. They were heavy and mocking in that way that videos of Nazis marching sounded.

Hamilton led me over to the guard hut and beyond.

Maxine glanced back at me for a second, and then back to her duty.

We cleared the exit barricades and walked out into civilian territory.

I felt like I was stepping out of prison for the first time in twenty years.

The black SUV was our destination. That was obvious.

As we neared the rear bumper, both front doors popped open. The driver's side door was pushed straight out and open by a man's arm.

The passenger side door was pushed open with a foot in a black heel and a short but attractive leg. It was a female, which was also obvious. The driver stepped out first.

He was a tall guy, but shorter than me. He had a lean look under a black suit and blue tie.

As he straightened up, he adjusted his coat. I saw the inside left side. He had a shoulder holster rig. Probably with a service weapon in it. The service being the FBI; I presumed because Hamilton had said Feds. Although I suppose that was common slang for the FBI, nothing said that it had to mean

FBI. It could also mean DEA or ATF or several other alphabet agencies.

The guy didn't wait for his partner. He shut his door and walked back to meet us.

The woman slid out the other side and closed her door.

She was a petite woman, also dressed in a black suit. No tie. And she wore a skirt. She had a white blouse; one button opened at the top. She wore a pair of gold rim sunglasses, slightly reflective, somewhere between a shiny surface and a mirror.

I watched her more than him because she was quite something. I like a woman in uniform.

She walked with a strut that was practiced by the time she was twenty, but it was perfected by the time she hit her thirties. And I presumed it was enhanced by a certain confidence that she had learned from being in law enforcement.

She had light brown hair. It was highlighted in a way that looked more like constant exposure to natural sunlight, rather than done out of a bottle in an overpriced salon somewhere.

Even though she was petite, fit, and on the right side of slim, she was no beanstalk. She walked with curves. The kind of natural curves that came from the right amount of nutrition, occasional sugar, and a whole hell of a lot of blessed genes.

I could see that she didn't have a shoulder holster rig, like her partner. I presumed she had a pancake holster at the small of her back.

Both stopped behind the SUV's rear bumper and stood there.

Hamilton walked closer, and I followed.

He stopped five feet from them, reached his hand out, and offered a handshake. First to the man and then to the woman.

He said, "Second Lieutenant Hamilton."

The man took his hand and shook it and said, "Agent Kelvin. This is Susanne Talbern."

They all shook hands.

No one introduced me, but Talbern looked me up, and down and back up. Which was fine by me because I was doing the same to her, but I had been doing it for alternative, carnal reasons.

She asked with a half-upward nod, "This him?"

Hamilton said, "This is the guy."

He reached into his front trouser pocket and pulled out a rolled-up, clear plastic bag. One downward flick of his wrist, and it cracked and unrolled itself.

The bag was ziplocked and marked as evidence on one side in big, bold, black letters, handwritten in black Sharpie, and not printed by the manufacturer.

There were no Army logos on it. No clear indications that it was an official forensic bag. Nothing like that.

My guess was that they had simply taken a ziplock bag out of the mess and repurposed its intended use, a simple makeshift evidence bag, just for me.

Hamilton said, "This is the tag."

Talbern continued to look at me. She said nothing.

Kelvin said, "Thank you. Lieutenant. You've done a good job here. The FBI appreciates it."

They shook hands, and Kelvin stepped over to me. He didn't touch me. He didn't reach out and take my arm like Coresca. He was more respectful and a hell of a lot more professional. He pulled out zip ties and asked me to put my arms behind my back to lock them on.

He said, "Sir, step this way. Walk toward the truck."

He pointed with an open palm at the back of the SUV.

I nodded and did as I was told.

I walked to the back of the SUV and then stepped past the back tire driver's side and stopped in front of the rear door.

I saw Talbern walk alongside me on the other side of the vehicle. Her hair was thick, even in the ponytail. It looked like it would jam up a woodchipper.

I winked at her, which I instantly regretted. Not sure why I did it. I realized to her it must've seemed menacing. I wasn't in handcuffs because of my charming personality. I was in handcuffs because they suspected me of something. And that something was bad if I was being handed over to the FBI.

Talbern didn't respond to the wink. She let it go, which I was grateful for, but the damage was done. I was sure.

Kelvin stopped behind me and opened the rear door.

"Get in."

I hopped in and sat on my hands and the cuffs. An uncomfortable feeling that I had before.

Before Kelvin shut the door, I stopped him.

I said, "Wait!"

He looked at me.

"They have my passport and bank card."

"We already got your belongings," he said and gestured toward a closed center console in the front cabin.

I nodded.

Kelvin shut the door and then hopped back into the driver's seat. He waited for Talbern to get in next. They shut their doors and buckled their seatbelts.

I guessed I wasn't getting one, which wasn't a surprise. I never did before. But every time I had been thrown into the back of a police vehicle before, I often had the same thought.

If Americans are always innocent until proven guilty, then why no seatbelt? Always made me think that was some subliminal indicator that we really are guilty until proven innocent.

I had no idea how this thought would be put to the test.

12

WE DROVE for less than an hour, back south. How I had come.

Finally, I asked, "Is someone going to tell me what the hell is going on?"

Kelvin looked at me in the rearview and said, "I'd like to."

He stopped there and thought for a moment. He stared at the road ahead and said nothing else.

I asked, "But what?"

He looked at Talbern, just a quick glance.

She turned in her seat, stared at me, and said, "We're not in the loop on what's going on. We're just escorting you."

"Escorting me? To where?"

Talbern said, "Orlando. The airport."

Orlando, I knew, because I had seen the signs.

I asked, "Airport? Where the hell am I going?"

They didn't answer that. Not with a destination, anyway.

Kelvin looked in his left-side mirror and flipped on his turn signal. He took us over to the left and to an off-ramp that led to the terminals.

He glanced back at me in the rearview and said, "You're going on a plane."

13

KELVIN AND TALBERN took me through a separate gate—separate from the rest of the airport traffic. It was for loading and unloading shipments.

I supposed I was the shipment.

The FBI skipped the departures and arrivals lines. No checking bags. No printing tickets. No conveyor belts for us. None of the usual hassles of traveling by plane.

I was going somewhere. The only perk was that it was on the FBI's dime. But I didn't know where they were sending me. I was positive it was nowhere that I wanted to go. Otherwise, having the FBI fly me to a new destination for free wasn't a bad thing.

The only thing was that it meant that they would know where I was. And the federal government knowing where I was; wasn't something that I was interested in. The sooner I could get them off my back, the better. The sooner I found out what the hell was going on, the faster I could go free.

The SUV slowed, and Kelvin showed his badge to a gate guard, who looked more former military than current airport security. He had that private military look.

Only one guard stood at the entrance to the loading section. Which made me think that if the guy was former military, then he was being over-utilized. But if he was washed up, then he was being used appropriately.

The gate itself was a chain-link gate on big rollers.

After the guard looked at Kelvin's badge and then a quick glance at Talbern and then me, he walked over to the gate and rolled it back, letting us pass through.

Kelvin thanked him and drove on.

The service drive led onto the tarmac, and the shift in asphalt was noticeable under the heavy tires of the SUV.

We bumped and split up and down for another five minutes, while Kelvin drove us beyond the tower and the nearest terminal.

We passed parked jets and baggage carriers snailing along on luggage towing vehicles that looked like converted golf carts. I wasn't sure what they were called. I had never been in the baggage handling business.

One guy towed a train of passenger luggage that looked like it was being taken off an Airbus. There were hundreds of checked bags. Mostly they were black. Occasionally, there was color sprinkled in.

My eyes immediately went to a pair of rucksacks. Military. There were probably for vets coming home from deployment. That was an experience that I had many, many times.

It wasn't an experience that I wanted ever to have again. Not that I didn't enjoy the Navy.

Navy life was what it was. Some good. Some bad. Like all military life.

But I had worked for sixteen years for them. Now I didn't work. Now, I lived on my own terms.

We drove beyond the parked jets and passed one large

runway. No planes were on it now, but the landing strip lights flashed and flutter to life as we passed it.

Kelvin ignored the lights and continued to circle around to the end of a large field beyond the runway.

At the end of the blacktop was a single white hangar. It was all lit up, and the doors were wide open.

The inside was empty of planes because the jet that was supposed to be parked inside was actually parked out front, nose facing the direction of the nearest runway.

It was a Gulfstream jet. It looked more like a private business jet rather than an FBI plane. I didn't care enough to identify the model type. It was a good-sized private jet, twin engines nestled out in front of the tail, stacked just above and behind the wings.

The turbines were spinning and humming.

The exit door was wide open, and the landing stairs were fully extended to the ground.

Two of the flight crew members stood out front. Both men. Both looked like pilots, but one might've been a flight attendant. I didn't see why the plane would need two pilots. But then again, why would it need a flight attendant for a passenger list of three people?

Kelvin parked the SUV in the hangar's mouth and killed the engine, left the keys in the ignition.

He and Talbern got out in the same manner that they had when I first saw them—Kelvin first and Talbern second. Like it had been rehearsed many, many times.

Kelvin opened my door and gestured for me to step out. He didn't grab my arm or give me attitude about it like Coresca would have.

Kelvin was much more professional.

I did as he asked and stayed quiet. No questions, because there was no point.

They had said that they knew nothing, and I believed them.

Kelvin led me over to the flight crew and shook hands with both men.

He said, "We're ready."

One man, the pilot, I assumed, said, "Let's board and take off."

We all got on the plane.

The chairs were all big tan, leather things that swiveled and rocked and reclined. Between them were small consoles with brown tabletops.

There was plenty of legroom.

Kelvin guided me over to a chair that was on the window, behind the wing, halfway to the tail.

"Take a seat, Widow. You'll get a good view from there."

I stared at the seat but didn't sit down.

Kelvin asked, "What's the problem?"

Talbern said, "His cuffs. Take his cuffs off. He won't sit on them."

Kelvin nodded and looked up at me.

The jet had relatively high ceilings. I could stand up tall, but the aisles were too tight for two people to stand side by side. I had to swivel around and look back at Kelvin.

I said to Talbern, "Thank you."

She smiled.

Kelvin said, "You going to behave?"

"Just put them on the front if you're worried about that."

Kelvin shrugged, and I realized they had never flown a prisoner before. That's why the Gulfstream looked like a jet for a private business. It was because that's exactly what it was. It wasn't a disguise. It was probably borrowed or rented by the FBI.

Which told me that whatever they wanted me for, it was

important if they were sparing no expense to fly me to wherever.

Kelvin took out the keys and uncuffed me and then recuffed me in the front. I nodded in a polite thank you gesture, which was more out of reflex than anything else. I wasn't thankful, because I was still pissed off that I was even in this situation.

That's what I get for trying to do the right thing.

After I sat, neither Kelvin nor Talbern sat next to me, which I had expected.

They didn't sit together either.

Talbern sat at the front of the jet, near the cockpit, and Kelvin sat all the way at the tail, last row.

The second guy from the flight crew had turned out to be a flight attendant because he walked over to me and told me to put on my seatbelt.

At first, he seemed professional and behaved normally. But then I lifted my hands and showed him the cuffs.

I asked, "How am I supposed to do that?"

He stared at me for a moment.

The cabin was calm around us. No sounds but the humming of the engines and then the steady rise of the noise as the pilot fired them up to get moving.

I hadn't tried to scare the guy, but suddenly he seemed a little scared.

He reached down for my seatbelt like he was going to strap it on me himself. But he hesitated halfway, like he realized I was a dangerous prisoner and not to be trusted.

He stopped.

I stayed quiet.

The guy flinched as a small hand grabbed him from behind.

I saw the fingers come over his shoulder. I saw the red painted nails.

Talbern asked, "What're you doing?"

The flight attendant said, "He needs to be wearing his seatbelt."

"Step aside," Talbern said, and they shuffled in the aisle and shifted and traded places.

She stepped into the row and leaned over me.

She smelled incredible, more like an attorney or a manager of a designer store over an FBI agent. Her ponytail cascaded down and fell over her right shoulder.

Her breasts were not in my face, but not far off.

The front of her blouse came open a little—only a little. But I could see enough. She had amazing breasts; that was clear. Slightly bigger than average. She was blessed with a serious display of womanhood. No doubt about that. No confusion on that point.

And then there were her eyes. They were some kind of green, crossed with some kind of blue, mixed with a hint of yellow. I wasn't sure what color to call them. Teal wasn't right, and to say they were turquoise was an understatement.

The best that I could come up with was immaculate. They were immaculate. Truly, a work of nature.

They were so mesmerizing that I forgot about my view of her breasts. And that was not in my nature. I am only a man, after all.

For a moment, we locked eyes as she reached down and grabbed my seatbelt. She pulled it over and across my waist and strapped me in.

Then she asked, "Is that too tight?"

I nodded and said, "No."

Which took me a second to realize that I had meant to shake my head, not nod it.

She smiled, stepped back and away from me.

"From now on, if you want to give him anything or need to adjust his seatbelt, don't do it without talking to me first."

She had spoken to the flight attendant.

He simply nodded and said, "You all should strap in. We're taking off."

He shuffled back to the cockpit.

Talbern said, "After we take off and it's safe, I'll come back and check on you. Okay?"

"I look forward to it," I said.

Instantly, I felt stupid about that. Beautiful women have a way of making a man say stupid things. I did not differ from any other man in that regard.

She gave me the same smile as before and turned and shuffled back down the aisle to the front row.

My feelings of embarrassment settled away after I thought about the fact that I was in handcuffs and she was an FBI agent. Saying something stupid was the last thing that was standing in my way of impressing her.

I settled back in the chair, which was about as comfortable as its first impression had made on me five minutes earlier. I'm not sure what type of chair it was called, but it was somewhere shy of a captain's chair, but certainly comfortable enough for a captain to use.

Everyone strapped into his or her seats. The flight attendant joined Talbern in the row at the front, and the jet started moving.

We nudged forward for about ten minutes—waiting. For what? I didn't know.

Whoever knows what's going on flights?

Finally, we ended up on a clear runway, and the jet amped to life. The wing's rear flaps creaked out and folded down, and the engines sprang to life like they had been simply humming in standby mode before.

For a small jet, the Gulfstream screeched and roared down the runway as loud and as aggressive as a large passenger jet.

In seconds, we were airborne and climbing the sky.

We flew north and away from Orlando, away from Cocoa Beach, and away from Florida, which was where I wanted to be. Already, my irritation with this whole thing was getting to me. The first part of my experience had been irritating, but at least I had been curious why a nameless dog tag had gotten me into this mess in the first place, but now I didn't care. Now, I was inching toward simply wanting off the plane and back to my peaceful life.

We flew on to a destination I wasn't sure about.

The flight attendant came around to me early on and asked if I'd like a snack.

Talbern stood behind him. She had seen him coming over and gotten up and walked with him.

I said, "I'd like some coffee."

She seemed to think for a moment, and then she shook her head in disapproval.

The flight attendant said, "Sorry."

"Then, I'm fine. Thank you."

He shuffled back and walked to the end of the cabin to Kelvin.

Talbern said, "Sorry, but I think that a hot cup of coffee on board a plane can be like a small, liquid grenade. Not a good idea to give it to you."

I nodded.

She paused a beat and then sat down in the chair next to me.

I was a little stunned.

She said, "I apologize for all the secrecy. We really got no idea what's going on. It's not our case. We were just told to pick you up and bring you..."

She stopped cold, like she wasn't supposed to tell me where we were going.

I nodded and said, "I guess we're going to Virginia."

She paused a beat, and then she said, "New York. Actually."

"I had a fifty-fifty shot that it was one or the other."

"I suppose you're right. We are headed north."

"And you're FBI. If you had been another agency, then I might've been off base."

She knew it was a simple deduction. I suspected she was playing good cop. But I said nothing about it.

If I had the choice between sitting next to the beautiful Talbern, versus not sitting next to her, I'd choose her every time. No question.

She looked forward to the flight attendant, who was staring back at us. And then he whipped his face toward the port side of the plane.

Talbern asked, "Who is Jack Widow?"

"Come on. You know who I am. Certainly, you've got my records by now."

"I saw your file, Widow. But there's a black tag on it. And it's a military black tag. Which means Special Forces?"

I stayed quiet.

"What I know is that you were in the Navy."

"That's all you know?"

"You grew up in Mississippi. I assume that must've been a small-town childhood. Your mother was a sheriff of a small town there. But she was murdered. I read you left the military while she was in the hospital."

She paused, swallowed, and said, "No one ever caught the guy who did it."

I asked, "They didn't?"

But I already knew the answer to that question. I had caught the guy.

She shook her head.

We hit a patch of turbulence. Talbern stayed cool as our seats rocked for a moment, and then everything calmed down.

She looked back at Kelvin. I assumed he shot her a suspicious look, showing anger at her for being so friendly with me, because she turned forward and stayed quiet.

15

THE GULFSTREAM GLIDED in over the tarmac for a long second. The landing gear touched down, and the wheels screeched. A temporary gust of smoke streamed up from the tires and whiffed away into the sky.

Talbern had stayed in the seat next to me, and the silence had stayed with her for the rest of the flight until we completely landed. The flight attendant made the announcement by telling us it was safe to remove our seatbelts and move about the cabin.

I got the impression that it was ten seconds after he told us he realized he didn't really need to. We weren't on a commercial flight, after all.

He did the whole song and dance out of habit, a sign of long instilled career programming like a retired baseball player accidentally trying to enter a stadium through the staff entrance rather than the public entrance.

Talbern smiled at me and said, "Okay, Widow. Let's go."

We exited the plane at another empty private jet hangar, same as before, only now it was completely night time, and this hangar was at JFK Airport. I was sure about that.

I had seen JFK many, many times.

Over the course of my career, I had stopped in the international terminal many times. Likewise, I had reentered American soil through the bureaucratic nightmare that was JFK's customs section for international travelers.

If I could remember all the times that I had to go through that process here, then it would be a number that was far into the double digits. Possibly even the low triple digits.

I could jokingly say that the number of free sky miles I would've racked up would've enabled me to fly for free for the rest of my life. The problem with saying that in a joking manner was that it might've been more of a truth rather than a joke. It wouldn't have surprised me.

Stepping off the last step of the landing stairs, Talbern tugged at my arm to follow her and Kelvin to another FBI SUV. This one was also black. Windows tinted. Big tires.

The difference in this one was that even though it was unmarked, it had a light bar on top. It wasn't an obvious big thing with big, round lights. This one was a thin, single bar, but it was plainly in view of anyone who inspected the vehicle. It wasn't embedded into the grille like most other official vehicles that I had seen before.

We were met by a single agent. He was a young, black guy who had an air of novice about him. He was a grunt; I assumed. He was only here to transport us to wherever we were going.

They put me into the SUV first. They buckled me into the backseat. They were nice enough not to make me sit on my hands, like before, and left the cuffs in the front.

Talbern ducked in over me and buckled me in.

The driver fired up the SUV, and we were off.

Even though I was no longer on Cocoa Beach, the heat in New York City felt as blistering as the heat in South Florida.

The whole Eastern Seaboard was going through record heat waves. I was sure that New York's proximity to the Atlantic Ocean added the right amount of humidity to the equation to help it feel like Miami heat.

During the sixty-five-minute ride across Brooklyn and into south Manhattan, we hit a steady stream of moving traffic.

The agent driving knew his streets well.

The bulk of Brooklyn was an easy ride for the time.

I leaned over and took a glance at the time display on the dashboard. It was seven-forty-seven in the evening when we arrived at the Federal Plaza on the corner of Broadway and Worth Street.

We passed around the front of the plaza. There were scaffoldings and thin metal constructs plastered across two side streets. Like most major cities, New York was under constant construction and changes.

Crowds of people walked in every direction. All of them had different destinations—hundreds, probably. But they all fell into a natural current, some going uptown and some headed down—people of all shapes and sizes, all different ethnicities, classes. There were people from all walks of life.

New York City was a city built from peaceful chaos.

I liked New York City. There was no place on Earth quite like it.

The driver stopped at a security gate on one of the side streets and smiled at a guard hut. The hut had tinted windows, but an open doorway. I saw two guys in there. One of them seated and punching keys on a keyboard. An old computer monitor flashed light across his face.

The other guard stepped forward and peered through the window.

He didn't bother to ask the driver to roll down the window. He waved us forward.

We drove into the building and down into an underground parking structure.

The driver didn't park. Instead, he drove us right up to an elevator hub and said, "You can go in here."

Kelvin said, "Where are we headed?"

"Tenth floor."

I followed behind Kelvin and into the elevator. We rode up to the tenth floor.

The doors opened, and I was shocked to find a lobby full of people.

Each of them stared at me with a shared-look on their faces.

They looked at me with expressions of both confusion and horror all at the same time.

16

TWENTY FBI AGENTS stared at me.

A black sign on the wall to the left, big and boxy, had white letters pinned to it. This was the New York FBI's Homicide Division, which made me realize I was in far worse shape than I had expected.

The people in the room appeared to have held their breath simultaneously as they waited for the elevator to arrive at their floor.

No one spoke for a long second.

Then a tall, slender man stepped forward. He had a face like a sundried prune and about the same amount of hair on top of his head.

But he had the opposite demeanor about him. He was the only person in the room to smile.

He reached his hand out for Kelvin to shake first.

They shook hands and greeted each other like long-lost friends, only it was all professional. Then he stepped over to Talbern and greeted her.

A woman stepped behind him. She was forty and not a day older or a day younger.

I could see muscular bulges in her arms under her coat. She had tanned skin and a tight neck, like she was in the gym every morning before breakfast.

She said nothing.

She didn't smile at Kelvin or Talbern, but she nodded to each of them.

She didn't look at me. There was something off-putting about it, like she was avoiding making eye contact with me on purpose. In fact, I sensed she was going above and beyond to avoid looking directly at me, which was weird.

I had never met her before, but I was getting a distinct impression that she hated me. It was worse than that, even.

The tall man stopped in front of me. He gave me a long look, up and down.

He didn't speak to me.

I finally spoke. I asked, "You like what you see?"

This didn't faze him like I had intended.

He said, "This way, gentleman."

Of course, Talbern wasn't a gentleman. He was referring to the three of us.

The tall man turned and walked through the crowd of FBI agents, and we followed. First was the woman who hated me, then Kelvin, then me, and Talbern taking up the rear.

I felt all eyes on me as I passed through the tunnel of people. We passed a reception desk that was empty and made our way down one short corridor. The slender man turned a corner and walked us halfway down a long corridor, past office windows and cubicles, and one large bullpen.

Computer monitors flashed, and FBI screensavers danced across screens like a rehearsed light show.

Every chair was empty because all the people who worked there had been in the elevator lobby, waiting for me like I was a local celebrity.

The slender man stopped and opened one door that was a set of double doors. We followed him into a conference room, one by one.

The conference room was all white walls, no windows—the complete opposite of the rest of the rooms on this floor that I had seen so far.

We crowded in, and the slender man said, "Have a seat."

He walked over to the front of the room and stayed standing. The agent who hated me followed behind him and stopped on the opposite side of him. She was holding the de facto evidence bag with the dog tag I had found in it.

Kelvin led me to sit at the far end of the table. He had pulled a chair out for me.

He and Talbern sat several feet behind me, near the door, leaving me seated at a long, oval conference table alone.

The slender man said, "Mr. Widow, my name is Raymond Pawn, and this is Kim Marksy."

I nodded and stayed quiet.

"Mr. Widow, do you know why you are here?"

I shook my head and said, "I'm sure you'll tell me."

"Agent Marksy was the special agent in charge of a task force about a year ago."

He looked at my face, watched my eyes, and my features, like he looked for some sign of recognition in them. There was none.

"Do you know what I'm talking about?"

I said, "I know what a task force is. I used to work in the military, which I'm sure that you know by now."

Pawn nodded and said, "She was in charge of a task force to catch AWOL."

I lounged in the chair, remained still. I didn't move. I didn't adjust.

Pawn stared at me.

Marksy stared at me for the first time. She had gray-blue eyes, deep-set blue like two cloudy sapphires.

There was hate laced in her eyes. I could see that she had an intense hatred for me or for whoever she thought I was.

There was something else there, too. There was confusion, I thought.

Pawn said, "No reaction, Mr. Widow?"

I said, "Should there be?"

"You've heard of AWOL?"

He was saying it like a proper name or a nickname.

I said, "I know what it means. I was in the Navy, as I'm sure you know."

"AWOL isn't a what."

I stared at him blankly.

"You really are going to play this game with us?"

I stayed quiet.

Pawn walked forward and slammed his knuckles down on the other end of the conference table. He leaned on them like a gorilla. He stared into me like a practiced interrogation move.

I kept his gaze, said nothing.

Marksy shifted behind him like she wanted a go at me.

"Look, guys. I really don't know what the hell is going on."

Pawn stood up straight and stared beyond me at Kelvin and Talbern, I presumed.

He said, "Agent Kelvin, would you get the lights, please. Just that first switch."

I didn't turn to look, but I could feel Kelvin's heavy footsteps as he turned and walked away from the wall behind me and over to the light switch near the door.

He flicked the first one on the panel, and half the lights in the conference room died away to black. Particularly, the lights over the wall behind Pawn and Marksy faded into darkness.

Pawn stepped out of the dark and over, halfway between me and the dark wall.

He scooped up a small black object. It was a remote to a projector that hung from the ceiling.

He clicked a button, and the small machine hummed and whirred to life.

He stayed in the middle of the room.

Marksy didn't move from where she was. She was at the edge of the shadows, near the back wall and the northeast corner of the conference table.

"Watch and see if you recognize any of your work, Mr. Widow."

I didn't like the sound of that, but I didn't protest. I just waited and watched.

Pawn clicked through a short series of introduction screens and clicked on a file marked "AWOL."

The first image that popped up was a photo of a young woman dressed in her Army uniform from graduation. An American flag was behind her right shoulder. She faced the photographer, didn't smile.

"Take a good look, Widow."

I looked.

"Recognize her?"

"No. Sorry."

Pawn kept his face squared toward the screen and clicked the next slide.

A new photo popped up. This was a different woman, but the same scenario. It was a black woman. She was young and attractive. An American flag draped from a flag pole behind her right shoulder. It was another graduation photo. She also wore her Army dress uniform.

I didn't wait for Pawn to ask.

I said, "I don't recognize her either.

Pawn clicked to the next photo.

"And this one?"

"Nope. Sorry."

"You don't recognize any of these women?"

"I already told you no. I have never seen them before in my life."

"You're sure?"

I nodded.

He clicked again and went to a photo of a man with a shaved head. No uniform. Not an Army graduation photo. This was a photo of a man in an orange jumpsuit. It was taken from the cover of an issue of *USA Today*. I could still see some of the title letters cut off at the bottom.

The man had been front-page news, whoever he was.

The print that remained in view about him was too small on the image to read.

"Recognize him?"

"Never seen him before."

Marksy finally spoke. She stepped forward and said, "You've never seen him?"

"I told you. No. I've never seen him before. I've seen none of them before."

Pawn asked, "You've never heard of AWOL?"

I didn't answer. I felt I had already answered that.

Pawn clicked ahead two slides. The images blurred past in a flash, like a blink of the eye. I couldn't make them out.

The new photo made me forget about them—quickly because it portrayed a gruesome scene.

The photo showed a dead, naked woman. She was stark naked and white as a sheet of paper.

There was no blood, but I was sure that it had been there.

I knew she was a woman because there were two breasts, plain as day and severed from the body just as plain. The skin looked like it had been hacked off in a violent rage.

Two craters, black and void, remained behind. The edges hacksawed and jagged stuck out to me.

The breasts were set aside on a steel slab at the woman's feet. She was on a morgue table; I presumed. The photo was well lit and had that sterile quality to it, like a doctor's operating table.

The body hadn't been autopsied yet, but I assumed this was just before that step.

She had one long leg—still attached. The other was there, but it was also detached from her body. It had been placed inches from where it should've been on the lower end of the table.

The photographer had gotten most of it in the frame. The tip of the foot of the missing leg was slightly out of frame.

The woman's face was there, but unrecognizable because it had been beaten to a pulp. Mashed eyes, crushed cheekbones, and a wrecked nose were all the features I could make out.

I heard Talbern make an audible sound, showing her shock.

I heard Kelvin shift his weight like he was looking away from the horror on the wall.

I stayed quiet. It was a horrible sight, but I had seen worse. However, I could see Marksy measuring my reaction like they expected me to be disgusted.

Pawn said nothing, clicked the button again, and the next

slide shuttered up on the wall. It was another dead woman—same as before.

Same cold, sterile look. Same metal table. Same morgue-looking backdrop.

Breasts lopped off. Right leg sawed off, just beneath the hip. And the face was bashed in and hammered to rubble.

There was a difference in this dead woman from the last. She was black.

I asked, "These are the women from the photos from before?"

Pawn said, "You already know that they are. Don't you?"

"What the hell is this?"

Pawn didn't answer. He clicked the slide show over to a third woman—same scenario as the previous two.

Then he clicked the slide show back several frames to the photo of the guy in the orange jumpsuit on the cover of the newspaper.

He didn't speak. He just studied my expression as I gazed upon the cold face of the guy in the photo.

Pawn asked, "You still going to act like you don't recognize him, Widow?"

"No clue."

Marksy stepped forward and said, "This is the guy we arrested. Know what for?"

"Killing those women?"

"Tell us about him?" Marksy said.

"I told you. I've never seen him before."

Pawn said, "This is AWOL."

Again, they both stared at me, waiting for a whiff of recognition on my face.

"AWOL is a serial murderer who killed three women last year. The three occurred eight weeks apart. Each of the victims was Army personnel. Each was roughly the same age.

Each was a similar build. Similarly, they were all very attractive."

Pawn paused a long beat.

I shrugged, not that I didn't care, but more like case closed. What does this have to do with me?

Pawn said, "The guy in the photograph is called Dayard."

This time, they got a reaction from me. I had heard that name before.

Marksy stepped forward and slammed her palms on the table, harder than Pawn had.

She said, "You know him!"

I said, "I've heard that name before. But I don't know him."

"You're lying!"

Pawn said, "The reason he's called AWOL is that each of his victims had more in common than just the fact that they were all young, beautiful women in the army. Each of them had abandoned her post at the end of her Army career. All three women had gone AWOL, and all three had been caught. They had all done their time in prison, and they had all been released sequentially."

Marksy said, "That wasn't enough for AWOL. So, he tracked them down and murdered them."

I stopped for a moment. Breathed in and breathed out.

I said, "So, this psycho killed three women. Their connection is that they all were former soldiers who went AWOL?"

Pawn said, "That's right."

I said, "So, Marksy was in charge of the task force that was supposed to catch him?"

Pawn nodded.

"And this guy was killing his victims inside of every eight weeks?"

This time both Pawn and Marksy nodded.

"Sounds to me like good police work. So, what the hell does this have to do with me?"

Pawn said, "That's what is bothering us, Mr. Widow."

"I don't understand."

"The name AWOL isn't a name that Dayard picked for himself. It was given to him by the media."

I nodded.

"The thing about choosing his victims because they all went AWOL is only part of it. There's one detail no one knows. No one but the agents on Marksy's task force."

I waited for him to tell me.

"AWOL did more than abduct and beat these women to death."

I stayed where I was and stared at him.

"This guy really hated these women. The bodies are bad. Truly the worst I've seen in a twenty-three-year career."

Silence. He studied my face, my eyes, as did Marksy. I felt her staring at me hard, like there was a map of the world on my face, and she had seen it before.

Pawn said, "The killer etched their names off their dog tags. Erasing them like they never existed."

I stayed quiet.

Marksy spoke like she was trying to correct me.

She said, "Like the one that you brought to us."

"I brought it after I found it."

"Where did you find it?"

"You already know that. I told Hamilton everything, already, back at Graham."

Pawn nodded, said, "You just found it in the sand on the beach?"

I nodded.

"That's a hell of a coincidence, Widow."

I shrugged, said, "Life is full of coincidences. Get used to it. It means nothing."

They stared at me.

I asked, "Look, I'm sorry about the dead women. Truly, that's an awful fate. But you have the guy. You already told me that. So, what the hell does it have to do with me?"

Marksy broke eye contact with me and looked at Pawn.

He stepped forward, halfway down the length of the table, the slide remote in his left hand. He clicked the button twice. The slides flashed in the opposite direction, across the wall, until the image stopped on the face of the man they had arrested for the AWOL murders.

Pawn said, "The thing is Widow that Dayard swears his innocence. In fact, he swears it to this day, even though his trial came and went ten months ago. Do you know where he is now?"

I said, "Prison?"

"Not just prison; he's sitting on death row. You see, one of the girls that was found, she was found on the coast of Portland. She was the first girl found. They're going to execute him, Widow."

I stayed quiet.

"The other thing is that you brought us a dog tag with the name etched out."

I nodded, said, "We already established that."

"Widow, we told no one about the dog tags."

I was silent.

Marksy said, "The newspapers were never told about the names missing from the dog tags."

Pawn intervened and said, "No one knew but us and the killer."

I stayed quiet.

Pawn said, "Dayard swears, he's innocent."

I asked, "And? What? You think I'm his accomplice or something? Just because I found a dog tag that someone scratched the name off?"

Marksy said, "The dog tag you brought us."

I looked at her.

"It's from a soldier who is missing."

17

THE LOOK on Marksy's face was somewhere between confusion and hatred, all while screaming severe distrust at me.

I got the feeling that she had a major discrepancy with my being here. For her, this was more than professional. It was personal.

Why she felt this way, I didn't know. Not yet, but I was certain that I would find out soon enough.

Before Pawn could say another word, Marksy pounded her fists on the table.

She asked, "Where is she?"

I stared at them, realized what was going on.

"Wait! You think I had something to do with AWOL?"

"A year ago, we made an arrest. We followed the clues. We caught a guy. But the guy claims to be innocent. Even now. And he's facing death. No getting out of that now. And here you are. You waltz in three days before he's being executed with a story about stumbling upon a new piece of evidence."

Marksy said, "Evidence that no one would know about except the real killer!"

Pawn said, "Or his accomplice."

"So what? You think that I'm his accomplice?"

"The girl who's missing was an officer. By all accounts, she was a good soldier. She went missing from Cocoa Beach. She was last seen by her sister on a Facetime call. She went down there to spend the weekend surfing. The same beach where you claim to have found her dog tag."

I stayed quiet.

Pawn asked, "Can you explain that?"

I said, "Look, I know nothing about a missing soldier. Certainly, I've got nothing to do with AWOL."

No one spoke.

I asked, "Has this woman gone AWOL? That's what you guys said was the killer's MO. But you just said she was surfing on a beach on the weekend. I presume she was off?"

Marksy said, "Her name is Dekker. Karen Dekker."

I shrugged.

Pawn nodded, said, "The dog tag is exactly the same."

"So, what do you think?"

"I don't know what to think, Widow. Dekker's been missing for a couple of weeks. You show up with her dog tag, scratched-off name. I'm thinking she's going to turn up dead."

I continued to stare at him.

"There's another issue."

I asked, "What's that?"

"You."

"How's that?"

"Who are you?"

Marksy interrupted. She said, "You have a Navy service record with the Department of Defense."

I nodded, said, "So?"

Pawn said, "So, you have two records."

I stayed quiet.

Marksy's face turned to more of curiosity than before, like a switch.

"Two files with the DOD. Why is that? I've never seen that before."

Marksy said, "I have."

Pawn looked at her.

"He was a double agent."

Pawn looked back at me and then at Marksy.

She leaned back from the table, crossed her arms.

She said, "What are you? A Navy SEAL?"

I didn't respond.

"Would his record be classified if he were a SEAL?"

Marksy said, "It would be, but there's more to it than that."

She looked back at me and asked, "Are you undercover?"

Pawn said, "Widow, if you don't help us, we can't help you."

"Help me with what?"

"You're helping him. Or you worked alone, but right now, it looks bad. We've got the son of a former Secretary of Defense on death row, who claims to be innocent, and now we have a potential break that may clear him."

Pawn said, "I don't want to send an innocent man to die. Help us, Widow. Tell us the truth."

"I told you the truth. I know nothing about the AWOL murders."

"Tell us who you are."

I thought for a moment and looked from face to face.

I said, "You don't want to know who I am. You want to know who I was. And you saw some of the information about who I was."

I paused a beat and said, "I was an undercover cop. That's

why my files are classified beyond classified. I was undercover with the Navy SEALs."

Kelvin interrupted with an involuntary gasp.

Pawn looked at him, over my shoulder, and then back at me.

He said, "How exactly did you do that? Did they pretend you were the cousin of someone in the SEALs?"

"No. I was a SEAL. In the Navy SEALs, you can't just waltz in and pretend to have been a SEAL that the guys never heard of. I lived a double life."

Pawn asked, "For sixteen years?"

I shrugged.

Marksy said, "Now what? You just wander around like a hobo?"

I nodded, said, "How long have you been an FBI agent, Marksy?"

She looked at me, then over to Pawn.

"A long time."

"I was in the Navy, four years, then I was NCIS for twelve years. When you get off work, are you still working?"

"Of course."

"But you go home to your family? Right?"

She said nothing.

"Not me. I went home to nothing. My team was my family. And I lied to them every day. I lied to them, but under the eyes of the law, I was the good guy. Know what it feels like to put your life in your teammates' hands?"

She nodded.

"Do you know what it's like to trust them with your life and then discover that they've sold secrets to a foreign government? Ever have to arrest someone who saved your life because you found out that he killed innocent people in order to cover up a crime?"

She said nothing.

"That's what undercover work is like. Every day you're told to investigate your friends. Every day you're expected to spy on them. In the end, you got to build a case about guys who, on the one hand, broke the law, but on the other, saved your life.

"So, yeah. I don't play by the rules anymore. I wander from place to place, doing what I want. I don't take orders anymore."

Silence.

Then I said, "That's what I did. I was an undercover cop. I lived a double life. And I'm sure that if you cross-check the murders with the Department of the Navy, you'll find plenty of alibis for where I was during the killings."

Pawn and Marksy looked at each other.

Pawn asked, "Anyone that I should call, in particular?"

"I can't give you that."

"How can we check this out?"

"Call OpNav and tell them the situation. Tell them who you are. I'm sure someone will report back fairly soon."

Pawn asked, "OpNav?"

"Office of the Chief of Naval Operations."

18

I WAITED in the conference room for about an hour while Pawn and Marksy checked out my story, which was quicker than I expected.

I never gave them the name of Unit Ten or Rachel Cameron, who had once been my commanding officer. Instead, I knew that if an FBI agent asked questions and bring up my name to the OpNav, someone would contact him to see what he knew.

And the contact from the OpNav would give just enough to clear me.

I sat and stared at a wall clock on the same wall where Pawn had shown the slides.

It was ten to six in the evening. I felt my stomach rumble. Which wasn't from being hungry. I figured it was from being still for so long. Eleven hours had passed since I first found Dekker's dog tags. I had been sitting around for most of that time. I wasn't the kind of man who sits around. I moved a lot.

I leaned back and swiveled in the chair, made eye contact with Talbern.

She sat upright, legs crossed, on a chair pressed against the back wall of the conference room. Kelvin wasn't there. I hadn't noticed, but he had left the room. We were alone.

I said, "Sorry to take you away from whatever you were working on in Florida."

She looked at me like I had broken her out of a trance.

"Don't worry about it. I've never been to New York before."

"You don't believe any of this, do you?"

She paused a beat and said, "I'm sure that I'm not supposed to comment on that."

"Come on. What difference does it make? You're just escorting me, right?"

"Guess you're right. No, I don't buy it. I'm more suspicious of the fact that you never heard of the AWOL killer."

"What do you know about it?"

"I didn't know about the dog tags. I remember it was about three years ago. They found the first body near a lake. They just showed up every so often."

"Was there a pattern?"

"They were all female. All went AWOL from their posts."

I wondered if they went AWOL or simply vanished.

I asked, "All Army?"

"Yeah."

"Same ranks?"

"No. All different. Were you really an undercover cop in the Navy?"

I nodded, said, "NCIS."

"So you're a civilian, then?"

"Depends on who you ask."

"What's that mean?"

"NCIS is ninety-five percent civilian."

She asked, "And the other five percent?"

I didn't answer.

Instead, I said, "I was sent undercover, so I had to be active duty at the same time. Otherwise, no one would buy into it. I always had to go all the way."

"My youngest brother is Navy. He wants to be a SEAL."

I nodded.

"Got any advice I can give him?"

"What kind of guy is he?"

She thought for a moment. Then she said, "He's a good soldier. Athletic. Strong. He's a real patriot type."

I nodded and said, "Sailor."

She said nothing.

"We're not soldiers. We're sailors. You call your brother a soldier; he'll tear you a new one," I said and smiled.

"Right. Sailor."

"Being athletic is a good thing, but what kind of guy is he?"

Talbern repeated he was patriotic, and then she added, "He's pretty hardcore. You know, tough. Like the kind of guys on our SWAT teams."

"What kind of person is he—mentally?"

"He's smart."

"How's his fortitude?"

She paused a moment and said, "Good."

Which was the right word, but the wrong answer because she had paused. Maybe he was a strong man with integrity and mental stamina, but that wasn't enough to get on the SEAL teams. He had to have the strongest of wills and the toughest fortitude to even get past the training. But I didn't tell her any of that.

I said, "Tell him to go for it. Can't hurt to try. The instructors will let him know if he's got what it takes or not."

She nodded.

Just then, Special Agent Pawn walked back into the room. He brought a new guy in with him.

Special Agent Marksy wasn't with them.

They approached me, the new guy behind Pawn.

Pawn stopped.

The new guy stepped around and stood behind me, which I didn't like.

Pawn said, "Jack Widow, I must apologize to you."

19

PAWN SAID, "We called the OpNav. At first, they denied knowing you or even ever hearing of you. Then, about thirty minutes later, the Assistant Director called me. My boss's boss. He told me to let you go immediately and prejudice. The Director of the FBI called him directly, and I can only guess who called him."

Probably, the Office of the Director of NCIS, I thought.

Pawn signaled to the agent that I didn't know with a nod, and he showed me a handcuff key.

He motioned me closer so he could unlock me, which I did.

He unlocked me, and I shook the cuffs off and let them fall to the floor.

No one picked them up.

I said, "I told you that you were wasting your time."

"Again, Mr. Widow, we are sorry. The FBI extends its apologies as well."

"Okay, don't get out of hand with that. I don't need sympathy."

Pawn nodded, said, "At any rate, I would like to speak to you further."

I backed up, stood up, and stretched my legs and arms.

Kelvin walked back into the room behind me. I heard the door open. I turned to see him. The look on his face, at first, was of panic, which made me realize no one had told him I was cleared.

He did nothing, just stayed there.

I turned my head back to Pawn and made eye contact again with the beautiful Talbern. This time, she smiled big. That made me feel pretty good.

"I've done enough for you guys already," I said.

"We know. And we appreciate that. But I really need to speak with you."

I nodded, said, "Go on."

Pawn turned to Kelvin and Talbern. He said, "Agents, you are dismissed."

Talbern asked, "Where do we go?"

Kelvin had already left.

"You're no longer needed. Good job. Return home."

I watched the disappointment on Talbern's face, which also made me feel good until I realized she might just be interested in the case. Her disappointment may have nothing to do with me, which made sense. To her, I was a has-been Navy cop and now a homeless drifter.

What the hell would a beautiful FBI agent want with a guy like me?

She took a last look at me and followed Kelvin out the door.

Pawn said, "Shut the door behind them."

He was talking to the agent who had freed me. The guy was younger than me. He was about six feet and built like a rock.

He walked to the door and closed it behind Talbern and Kelvin.

He didn't return to the table. He stood at the door like a secret service agent.

Pawn sat at the left side of the table and motioned for me to return to my seat. Instead, I moved to the seat across from him. I wasn't keen on sitting in the same place that he wanted me to be. I hated to go where they told me to go. The natural rebel in me was always rebelling.

"Widow, I really am sorry for suspecting you."

I nodded, said, "You already apologized. Let's move on."

"I just want you to understand that the AWOL murders took a toll on this office. We worked very hard to catch him. For months, this entire office was exhausted. We were the central task force."

"Agent Angela Marksy was the lead agent."

I nodded.

"She's not happy that after a lot of grueling police work and the sacrifices that she made, that you come along and throw a wrench in everything."

"Sacrifices?"

Pawn looked at the other agent over my shoulder and back at me.

He sat forward as if to show that we were now speaking in a private bubble.

"Agent Marksy lost her partner, trying to catch AWOL. Around two years ago, Marksy and her partner had locked AWOL into a corner. They tracked him to a throwaway apartment in White Harbor, Maine."

The florescent lights quietly hummed above. In the north end of the room, the air vent kicked on. The humming sounds joined in a slow, sedative purr. I wasn't sure if that was productive for an FBI office.

Pawn said, "Agent Marksy and Agent Lowe were more than partners. They were married."

I looked at Pawn. Things made a lot more sense.

I said, "No wonder she hates me."

"Right. She has just started to put this whole thing behind her. She wants to see Dayard fry, as we all do. Honestly. But now you come along with evidence of another murder victim."

"We don't know that. There's been no crime beyond defacing Army property."

He nodded.

"What now?"

Pawn said, "Now, I'd like to ask you to help us out."

"What can I do?"

"To be honest with you. There's another component."

"What?"

"I've been instructed to ask you to remain with us for the night."

"What other component?" I asked again.

"I think it's best if you wait and see for yourself."

I looked at the wall clock again.

I said, "It's getting late. Where do I stay?"

"We'll put you up in a hotel. In the morning, someone will come for you."

I spent a little time thinking it over because Pawn had me boxed in, and he knew it.

Where was I going to go?

I was far from where they had found me. I figured that was his thinking. I could've just left. Nothing really was stopping me.

But I stayed.

"I've not been to the city for a long time. Why not?"

"That's the spirit," Pawn said, and he turned back to the other agent, waved him over to us.

The guy walked over and stopped five feet from me.

Pawn said, "This is Special Agent Gustoph. He'll escort you around. Anything you need, you ask him."

I nodded and stood up and shook his hand.

Gustoph had a strong grip.

"Good to meet you, Widow."

I looked him up and down and asked, "You're former military?"

"Yeah. I was a Marine."

I nodded, said, "Marines are good."

"Damn right."

"Pawn, can I speak with you alone?"

"Sure."

Gustoph walked back to guarding the door.

Pawn waited for me to speak first. I said, "Look, you want my help?"

"I do. We need to find out the connection before Dayard goes to the chair."

I nodded, said, "Then I don't need this guy to babysit me."

"Widow, you need someone with you."

"Why not Talbern?"

"Agent Talbern belongs in Jacksonville. Not here."

"Let her babysit me. I don't know any of you, but she was nice enough to me. Trust me. I can work with her."

Pawn thought for a moment and said, "You take both. I can live with that."

I shook my head, said, "Make it Kelvin and Talbern instead. They're already both in this together."

"Okay, fine. You take them both. I'll call them back."

"This will work much better than some former military hard-ass. Trust me."

I was mostly telling the truth. I had nothing against Gustoph, but he was a straight-up military man. I had seen his kind thousands, millions of times. I knew his kind. Nothing wrong with them, but I needed someone who could help me investigate this, not someone to babysit me.

Both Kelvin and Talbern had already proven themselves to be respectful, honorable, and seemed like good investigators.

Plus, a part of me wanted to see Talbern more. I figured that there was nothing wrong with that.

Pawn pulled out a cellphone and dialed a number. He stepped away for a moment and came back over to me. The cellphone had gone back into the pocket of his trousers.

"Widow, head back outside and take the elevator down to the lobby. Don't worry. Security is expecting you to pass through. Go out to the curb and past the gate. They'll pick you up there."

I nodded.

"They're going to check you into a hotel. Here. Take this with you. It's unlocked."

Pawn handed me a small tablet. It was thin and sleek. One of the newest versions of the iPad, I figured.

"Study the files on the AWOL case. They're all on the desktop. Learn up on it and get some sleep. Tomorrow, we've got a lot of work to do."

I thanked him and walked past Gustoph, who grinned at me like he was taking it personally, which I was sure he was. But I didn't care.

I followed Pawn's instructions and zigzagged back the hallways, alone and back to the elevators. No-one stopped me, but everyone stared.

I took the elevators down to the ground floor and was greeted by a single security guard who introduced himself and took me out of the building, to the gate on a side street and then waited with me for a long, silent minute while Kelvin and Talbern pulled up to the sidewalk curb in an SUV that was smaller than the one we drove in back in Florida.

Still, it was black and unmarked but had police lights embedded into the grille in the front and a collection of small radio antennas on the roof.

I smiled at Talbern, who I believed was happy to see me as well. I got in the back seat, and Kelvin asked, "The FBI has a list of pre-approved hotels. Wanna hear them?"

I said, "No. Take me to the most expensive one."

Kelvin reached up and adjusted the rearview, looked at my eyes.

He asked, "You used to that kind of life?"

"I've been sleeping in motels, train stations, bus depots, and occasionally under overpasses for the last several months. I think a good hotel in New York City sounds nice for a change."

"Especially on the FBI's dime, right?" Kelvin asked jokingly.

I smiled and said, "The taxpayer, actually. So it's just as much my money as it is theirs."

Talbern craned her head, looked at me with those eyes. She said, "I thought you don't pay taxes."

I smiled and said, "Exactly."

20

THEY PUT me up in the George Hotel on the Upper West Side. The hotel was fitted in between two apartment buildings, with retail space at the bottom on Riverside Drive. The George faced the river and had a pretty good view.

My room wasn't facing the river. I had a single room with a small window facing down into a courtyard, shared with another property to the east.

The first thing that I had noticed when we checked in was that Kelvin and Talbern did not share a room, which was what I wanted.

They were partners. More often than not, that kind of professional kinship can lead to romantic involvement. Pretty standard. I had seen it many times in the military.

That's the main reason for all the military codes of conduct regarding fraternization and improper relationships among officers and their crew members.

In every branch of the military that I was familiar with, it was not only frowned upon to have sexual or romantic interactions between the ranks, but it was also illegal and could lead to punishments beyond that of simply being terminated.

Most situations could carry with them jail time. And military prisons were no fairytale world.

Military prisoners often were jealous of civilian prisoners who had cushy mattresses and special privileges and government protections of their constitutional rights.

They were lucky compared to military prisoners.

Even with strict punishments, people were people, and relationships happened. And they happened at all levels.

The Navy was susceptible to romantic incursions because a lot of sailors—male and female—were stuck at sea together for long periods of time.

Nothing promotes unlikely relationships more than being stuck in solitude together for months on end.

I can't say that I hadn't been a victim to this temptation myself.

Talbern and Kelvin weren't in a relationship, which was all I really wanted to know.

After we checked in, they led me to my room, and I stayed there for a while. I took a shower, left my clothes on the bed. They were new, but I had worn them all day, including on a plane ride. I thought about sending them out for laundry service.

The question wasn't about whether the George Hotel offered such a service. I was in New York, in a hotel, on the Upper West Side. Of course, it offered a laundry service.

The question was, what would I wear while I waited? Simple answer, I found in the bathroom. Two expensive-looking bathrobes were folded up tight on a shelf underneath the sink.

I smiled at first because I thought of one being there for Talbern to use.

So, I stripped down and hopped in the shower.

The shower was a big glass box that took up an entire

wall. The glass stretched from floor to ceiling. It was a nice shower.

There was a rainforest showerhead hung over the center of the shower. And onetime use shampoos and conditioners and a bottle of body wash that could be used twice. No wash-cloths. There were only folded large bath towels, and a couple of hand towels hung from stainless steel rings on either side of the sink.

After I showered, I wiped the steam off the mirror and looked myself over. The first thing I noticed was a few patches of gray hairs along my temples and in the stubble on my face.

First signs of an aging man, I thought.

I walked out of the bathroom and felt myself getting hungry. I kept the robe on and left it open. The clothes from Florida were laid out over the bed.

The bed was a king-size. The head was blocked by a plethora of stacked pillows, and the bed's coverings were tight and pressed and neat. I dumped myself down on the corner and reached over to the nightstand. I scooped up the iPad and looked over the AWOL case.

There had been three dead women, plus the new one if she was dead.

I spent about twenty minutes scanning over the material that Pawn had provided.

Four dead women. Four dead soldiers. All-female. All beaten with a hammer. All shot in the head. All were dumped along the Portland coast of Maine.

That part I hadn't known before.

I read on further. I found Marksy's notes.

She had conducted a solid case, building a profile on the AWOL killer.

I read about the first victim in the most detail.

Hers was the first file that I came to. She had been

found on the shore of the Atlantic. The nearest town on a map had been called Butler, for reasons that weren't clear to me.

She had been found by two boys in a long patch of forests.

I read over their testimonies. Brutal stuff for two young boys to see.

I read on to the next victim. It was the same story, found in Maine. She was found two months later. Her head had been shaved, and she was a black woman. But everything about the cause of death, the torture before death, the dog tags; all of it was there.

After her, I skipped ahead and skimmed the last one. Everything seemed the same. The only details that each woman shared, other than the last moments of their lives, were that each had been female, and each had gone AWOL from her post.

I swiped through more of the details of their lives and went straight to notes of the case. These weren't the same as Marksy's notes.

Her notes had been typed in great detail. She mentioned everything about what she had seen all the way down to the colors of locations and times that were marked down to the minute.

The new pages of notes that I came to were different. Less detailed. More to the point. Big picture stuff.

I read they were from an agent named Chris Lowe.

He must've been the agent that Pawn had mentioned. Marksy's husband and longtime partner.

Speaking of relationships and fraternizations, I guessed the FBI didn't have rules about such a thing if a husband and wife could be partners. Then again, I guessed that it all depended on the circumstances.

An investigative team wouldn't raise any eyebrows or kick

up enough fuss to warrant separation of the pair, especially if they were getting results.

Lowe's notes ended with suspicion of a suspect. They had targeted a guy named James Dayard.

He had been an Army officer, who made it all the way to major.

Major Dayard had been linked to one of the women. Socially. And later, romantically. The first victim had been a married woman. What Marksy and Lowe found out was that she had broken up with Major Dayard, and then she had gone AWOL.

According to Marksy's notes, the Army MPs thought she was AWOL because she vanished the day that she was supposed to get on a flight to Germany for a tour.

Later, the other women started vanishing from their posts. Each turned up dead.

That's when the FBI connected them as all being women targeted for going AWOL.

Marksy believed the killer etched their names off their dog tags as a symbol of their treason. She believed he felt betrayed by them.

I imagined that made much more sense after they caught Dayard, connected to him and the first woman.

On paper, it made sense to me. A scorned officer. An illegal affair. The woman ended it. Dayard felt betrayed and resented. So he tortured her and killed her.

I read on.

There was also an official psychological profile in the files about Dayard. A military shrink found him to be disturbed, but couldn't make any analysis of if he was guilty.

I paused for a second and then heard a knock on the door.

I got up, walked over to the door.

"Who's there?"

"It's me. Talbern."

I smiled, unlocked the deadbolt, but stopped. I closed the robe first, looped the rope belt around, and knotted it.

I opened the door and said, "Hey."

She stood in the doorway, shrouded in the kind of confidence that belonged on a senior FBI agent, but was to be expected on a woman who probably never heard the word *no* to anything.

Her hair was no longer pulled back. It hung down, curtaining the sides of her face. Her ears were swallowed up in it and were completely covered. I could've compared them to something lame, like a flower, but they were just as close to the thorns of a rose as they were to the beauty of one. She looked dangerous and seductive, like a rare firearm. For a guy like me, a rare gun is a beautiful thing, but it's still a weapon.

Talbern was deadly. I wondered why Pawn hadn't assigned her to me over that stiff, Gustoph. I was more likely to cooperate with Talbern around. What man wouldn't?

She had changed her clothes. Even though her hair was down, her clothes had changed to reflect comfort over style.

She wore black jeans, tight and faded in the way teenagers spend a fortune on.

She kept the same jacket from earlier. But underneath it was a low-cut red shirt. I could see the tops of her breasts just enough to draw my attention, but professional enough to be called causally conservative.

Then I noticed she was armed. The shoulder rig was virtually hidden under the jacket, except for a brief second when she looked at me and folded her arms.

She said, "Well, aren't you living it up in here."

"What?"

"You look like a man who is enjoying a spa day."

I looked down at the bathrobe.

"I took a shower."

"Just now?"

"It's been a while."

"So then you're just hanging out in the bathrobe?"

I shrugged.

"What are you doing?"

"I was looking over the case. The old stuff."

"That's good, but I mean, what are you doing tonight?"

I stared at her blankly. Then said, "Going to bed."

She unfolded her arms and said, "Widow, it's eight-thirty."

"That seems like a normal time that people go to bed? Isn't it?"

"We're in New York City."

I shrugged again and stayed quiet.

"It's Friday night."

"Is it?"

"You lose track of the days?"

"Sometimes. There's no reason to keep track of them for me."

"I guess not."

Talbern reached up and touched the robe just over my left pectoral. She nuzzled me aside and walked into the room.

I didn't object.

"Let's go out."

"Go out?" I felt my stomach rumble again, but this time I was certain it was more out of being nervous over being hungry.

"Yeah. You gotta eat. You haven't eaten, have you?"

"No."

Talbern looked at the bed and then back at me. She said, "Crap. You only have those clothes. Right?"

"That's it."

Talbern sat herself down on a chair near the window. She said, "There's a store in the lobby."

"Will that be open?"

"Right," she said, and then she pulled out her cellphone.

She stared at the screen, swiped it unlocked, and clicked on a couple of buttons. She wasn't dialing, but redialing someone.

She put the phone to her ear and waited.

"Hey. You got a change of clothes?"

I couldn't hear the voice on the other line, but I imagined it was Kelvin.

"Good. Let me borrow them."

She listened and then smiled and laughed and said, "Not for me. For Widow."

She was silent again, listened.

"I'm a big girl. Just let him borrow them."

She clicked off the phone, said, "You'll have clothes in five minutes."

I nodded.

She slipped the phone back in her pocket and looked over at the tablet from Pawn. She got up off the chair, and walked to the bed, picked it up. She swiped through it.

"Did you already go through the whole thing?"

"Enough."

"You read about Lowe?"

I nodded.

"Agent Marksy doesn't like that you're here."

"A stranger shows up after she has put a killer away with evidence that possible he didn't do it. I imagine not."

"You think he's innocent?"

I shrugged, said, "We don't know that. All we have is a new set of dog tags. Means nothing."

"Looks the same as before."

"Maybe. But the other bodies were found with the dog tags around the victim's neck."

She nodded.

"Where's the body?"

She said nothing.

"We need to find Dekker."

A knock on the door interrupted us. I stood up, and Talbern stood up. She walked to the door ahead of me. She opened it.

Kelvin stood in the doorway, still wearing his suit from earlier, but no jacket. His gun was gone, or it was in his pocket.

"Come in," she said.

He walked in and had a pair of black slacks folded, with a white button-down slung over it. The shirt had no hanger but was wrinkle-free, like he had just pulled it off a hanger. Or maybe he ironed it for me, or for himself, the night before he wanted to wear it.

She took the clothes and said, "Thank you."

I nodded at Kelvin. He handed the clothes to her.

"What about shoes?" she asked.

Kelvin looked at her, said, "He doesn't have shoes?"

"He can't wear this with sneakers."

Kelvin nodded and walked over to the vanity, leaned against it with one hand. He used his free hand to loosen one shoe. He kicked it off. Then he did the other one. He bent down and picked them up, held them by the heels, and handed them to her.

In a playful tone, he asked, "Anything else for you, princess?"

She tilted her head and said, "No, thank you."

I didn't have any socks to wear with his shoes, was my first thought. Then I wondered if we even had the same shoe size.

But I stayed quiet.

Talbern turned to me and handed me the clothes. She said, "Get dressed and meet me by the elevators."

I nodded, watched the two of them walk back out the door and into the hall.

They seemed pretty close. I wondered if they had ever been involved before. Probably. I didn't ask.

I watched the door close behind them, changed into Kelvin's spare clothes, and slipped the shoes on. They were a little snug, but fit good enough. My feet weren't cramped in them. I wouldn't be playing any basketball in them, but then again, they weren't athletic shoes. They were black loafers. Dressy enough to look professional, but comfortable enough to run in.

I had never been an FBI agent, but if I remembered correctly, they were required to run up several flights of stairs without being winded. A part of the job meant being able to have a successful foot pursuit. Can't let bad guys outrun them, even on stairs.

The shoes were a little extra uncomfortable without socks. And the thought occurred to me that Kelvin might not like that I wore his shoes barefoot, but what he won't know couldn't hurt him.

I stood in the bathroom and looked at myself in the mirror. I tucked in the shirt. I had no belt to wear, but the shirt kept the pants up enough. The waist size on them was about right for me, anyway.

The shirt's sleeves were too small. Other than that, I looked pretty decent.

I rolled the sleeves up over my forearms. I left the bathroom, walked over to the vanity, and scooped up my bank card, passport, and hotel room key. I slipped everything into my front pocket.

Before I left, I stopped and stared at my toothbrush. This one wasn't foldable like the ones that I prefer to carry. I left the toothbrush. Why would I need it just to go out for dinner?

I stopped in the doorway because I felt a little naked without it. Toothbrushes have been one of the few things that I carried regularly.

Realizing that I wouldn't have one on me made me feel a little awkward.

I stopped and turned back and scooped it up. Put it into my other pocket. It stabbed me in the thigh for a second until I adjusted it.

I walked out the door.

21

WE TOOK an Uber and not a cab, which was strange for me, to a lounge about a half-mile away. Not that far, but Talbern didn't seem like she wanted to walk there.

The bar served Hawaiian style food, but the décor of the place was anything but Hawaiian. It was a posh modern place with ambient blue lights that reflected the walls. The ceilings were high, and there was a second-floor mezzanine with high-top tables spread around it.

The floors were polished concrete. They were completely smooth and level.

People filled the place up just enough to take up most of the seats, but it wasn't crowded.

I was a little surprised that it wasn't packed because the bar looked like the kind of place that New Yorkers would love.

We sat at the bar, back wall, near the kitchen.

Low jazz music played over speakers along the bottoms of the walls. There was a small stage off to the other side of the bar, but no musician was there. The music was probably playing from someone's smartphone.

Talbern had to use the foot-bar beneath the bar to hop up onto the seat.

I dumped myself down in the seat next to her.

She ordered a martini, which didn't surprise me. I got the sense that it wasn't her drink of choice. Instead, she had that kind of adventurous spirit of a person who always tries new things—that kind of "when in Rome" attitude.

The martini was something off the menu, a creation of the lounge. Maybe even of the bartender that we had.

Our bartender was a woman who looked so young that she might've been a girl. But I suspected that to bar tend in the state of New York; she had to be twenty-one or eighteen.

Besides looking young, she was professional and personable, and not talkative.

I ordered a Budweiser at first, but Talbern gave me a look. I changed it to a Heineken, which seemed to please her enough.

Talbern sat, legs uncrossed, knees together, even though she wore jeans. Her back was up straight, not touching the back of the stool, which triggered a childhood experience that I had. Long ago, my mother had taught me to be what she called a gentleman. A gentleman was more than just social behavior and manners. She always corrected me to sit up straight, elbows off the table, don't slurp my drink, and so on.

Talbern's perfect posture without leaning back in her chair made me wonder which of her parents had set that kind of behavior into her psyche. Maybe it was a grandmother or an aunt. Or maybe it was a mother like mine.

I smiled at her.

She took a measured sip from her martini and made a yummy sound.

"That's good."

"Mine too."

"Of course, it is. Heinekens don't change flavor."

"Not true," I said.

She said nothing.

"They make Heineken Light."

She smiled, said, "Heineken Dark too."

"Really? I never heard of that one."

"You gotta get out more, Widow."

"Are you kidding? I am always out."

"I know. It's called a joke."

I took another pull from the beer and looked away from her at the back of the bar.

Several assorted shelves of liquors lined the back wall. There was a dust-free mirror behind it with a large etched phrase. It read: *Drink till it's good!*

Beneath the shelves was a back bar with all the things one would expect to find: cutting boards, shaker tins, jiggers, and so on.

Below that was a long row of slider doors. All were glass. That's where they kept all the beers and cold beverages.

In the mirror, I could see most of the rest of the patrons in the bar. There were high-top tables near the bar. I saw on a lower level a series of dark booths and a row of tables. Just about everything was filled up.

I saw waitresses and a manager walking around frantically, as lounge staff often do on a Friday night.

* * *

WE ORDERED two more rounds each over the course of the next hour. We talked the whole time and snacked on bar nuts.

About a half-hour into our conversation, a couple of things happened, I noticed. First, a guy with a saxophone stepped into the lounge from out of the kitchen's entrance. He walked by us and stopped to converse with a group of people who sat at the other end of the bar. Then he shook hands with them and grabbed a drink from the bartender.

He walked onto the stage and played the saxophone, close to the microphone. He continued to play jazz. Occasionally, he would stop and say something over the mic. People in the lounge clapped after every set.

I figured that some of them were fans of his, and others had never heard of him.

The second thing that happened, just after he started playing, was a guy walked in who didn't belong. But I said nothing to Talbern because I wasn't on the job anymore. A guy who walks into a bar and sticks out to me has nothing to do with me.

The first thing about him that stuck out was his clothes. The guy wore sunglasses, a worn black suit, black tie, and slacks to match. Not to mention the tiny white earpiece that came out of his shirt collar and ran up to his ear.

He looked like Secret Service, but that made no sense. What the hell would a Secret Service Agent be doing in here, alone? Unless he was giving the place a security audit. Maybe he had a protectee coming by later.

The best I could figure was that the guy was scoping the place out for that reason.

He took his sunglasses off and sat at a dark booth. His face fell out of sight when he sat back into the shadows.

I got a second glance at him, with the sunglasses off, when a waitress came over to take his order.

I couldn't hear them, but I watched as she took his order and smiled. Then she returned later with a tall glass of something that looked like soda water.

Occasionally, the guy leaned forward to take a drink.

A little voice in my head, which reminded me of Rachel Cameron's voice, was telling me to keep an eye on him.

I turned back to Talbern and tried to forget about the stranger.

She told me some personal stuff about herself. She was divorced, going on six months now. The guy had worked in an airport or been a pilot or something like that. She was vague about what he did for a job. But she was much more forthcoming on what he did to piss her off.

The guy had cheated on her with their neighbor. This had all happened in Tennessee. She had only been in Florida for six months.

After she caught them, she packed her stuff and took a transfer.

I asked her how she got it so fast. She told me they had been asking her to go for weeks. Like the military, the FBI likes to move its people around every once in a while. They don't like their agents to get complacent.

They like them sharp, on their toes, and ready. Understandable.

I asked, "What's the story with you and Kelvin?"

Even though she had been sitting straight the whole conversation, she suddenly seemed to tense up, like I had hit a nerve.

"Why? Nothing's going on. Kelvin is married."

"I wasn't implying anything. Just asking. It's normal in the Navy for two people, partnered together, to be attracted. Happens every day."

She was quiet.

"You two seem to have a good relationship."

"We're friends. That's it."

I stayed quiet.

She said, "I mean."

She paused, like she was contemplating the thought. Then she said, "I hit on him once. In the beginning. I tried to kiss him. We had gone out for a drink."

Like this one, I thought.

"Believe me. I was embarrassed about the whole thing."

"What happened?"

"Nothing. I told you. He's married."

"He turned you down?"

She nodded.

"I'm sorry. But no way!"

"You don't believe me?"

"I believe you. I mean, there's no way I would've turned you down."

"He's married."

I said, "He's a better man than me. I wouldn't have been able to resist."

"I saw his wife. She's beautiful."

"Wouldn't matter to me."

"You'd cheat on your wife?"

"I'd like to think not, but then again, I never imagined a woman like you out there."

She smiled, pressed a finger up to her lip like she was contemplating chewing her nail, but resisted. Temptation. Right there in front of me.

She asked, "What if your wife was Marilyn Monroe?"

"Even if my wife was Rita Hayworth."

"Who?"

"She's a movie star. Before Monroe. And a lot more beautiful."

"I like Marilyn."

"Nothing wrong with her. I'm just more partial to a classy woman."

Talbern laughed out loud. She said, "You? Classy?"

"What's wrong with me?"

She laughed a little harder, almost too hard. I thought she was picking on me more than actually laughing.

She rested her hand on my knee. And I noticed.

"I'm sorry. Sorry. You are a classy guy."

"I can be."

"I'm sure."

I smiled at her again and examined my bottle. It was near the bottom. So was her martini.

I asked, "You want another?"

She slowed her laugh and looked at her drink. Instead of answering me, she let go of the stem of the glass and reached into her pocket. She pulled out her phone, looked at the screen.

"It's getting late. We should head back."

"What time is it?"

"Ten to midnight."

"We should get back to the room."

I perked up because she'd said room and not *our* rooms. Not that it meant anything. But I liked the implication that came with it. A guy can pretend.

"I'll get the check," I said.

"Nonsense. I'll get it."

I paused a moment, and then I said, "Nah. I should pay. I'm a gentleman, remember?"

"I know. But let me pay. It's the FBI's money. Not mine."

I shrugged. It sounded good to me. But she must've felt the need to sell me more on it because she added, "The way I see it, they owe you. They plucked you out of Florida and sent you here in handcuffs. The least they can do is pay for your drinks."

I nodded and said, "They already paid for my hotel room."

"True."

"Plus, the flight here. Really, the FBI has paid for me to have a vacation in New York. Not bad in my book."

"That's a good way to look at it."

Talbern leaned forward on her stool and asked the bartender for the bill.

After she gave the girl her card, she sat back and said, "I'm going to go to the lady's room."

I nodded.

"When the bill comes back, just sign it. Leave a tip."

"I always do."

She took her purse with her and swiped her left hand across my shoulders on the way to the restroom.

I smiled. Then I thought about the amount of trust she was showing me by leaving her card.

I waited. The bill came, and I signed for it, took the card, and left a fifteen percent tip.

I drank the rest of my beer and set the bottle down on the bar.

The bartender took both drinks and the bill away and thanked me for the tip.

I waited a little longer.

The musician played one more set and then stopped. He said that he would return after a short break. I turned in my seat and faced the stage; then, I glanced at the bathrooms. She still hadn't come back out.

I looked over the crowd. The Secret Service agent was gone.

That startled me for a moment because I hadn't noticed that he had left. Then again, I wasn't supposed to notice. It was his job to be invisible when he needed to.

This got me thinking. If he was good enough to slip out without me noticing, then why did he make himself visible to me when he came in?

I shrugged to myself and glanced back at the bathroom doors.

There were a women's and a men's bathroom. Both were clearly marked. Black doors. On a black wall.

Suddenly, one of the doors opened. It wasn't the woman's. It was the men's. A bright white light washed over a table nearby. A pair of couples sat there. They didn't look back at the restroom light.

A short, fat man walked out. He was still drying his hands on a paper towel. Before the door shut behind him, he chucked the paper towel back into the room. Probably into a wastebasket that was out of my sight.

I waited.

The bartender came back around and asked if I needed anything else.

I told her no, but I asked for the time. She said it was about midnight, not midnight, but *about midnight*, which meant that it was probably five past.

Talbern had gone in at ten to midnight, and now it was about five past. She had been in there for over ten minutes. That length of time might've been regular for a woman to do at home, but not in a lounge.

I should'

I needed to pee anyway, so I thought I'd better check it out.

I stood up and walked across the room, around the bar, to the bathrooms.

I went into the men's room, closed the door.

It was a single-person bathroom. There was a toilet, a sink, and a urinal on the wall, but there was no stall. I locked the door and used the urinal. Then I washed my hands.

As I twisted the knob on the faucet to turn off the water, I heard a sound in the women's room. I paused and listened.

It was the sound of running water. Talbern had been washing her hands.

I dried mine and walked out of the bathroom.

A man dressed in a shirt and tie stood there. He had a thin mustache and a bald head—no trace of hair anywhere.

He smiled at me and scooted past me into the men's room like he couldn't wait to use it another second.

I stepped out and stayed near the doors.

I waited for Talbern to come out.

The women's door opened, and a woman stepped out. It was a woman who wasn't Talbern.

She must've been startled to see me because she jumped back and grabbed at her chest like she was having a fast heart attack.

"Sorry to scare you, ma'am."

She took a breath.

The woman was older. She was probably in her late fifties. She had a short, thin body. She was dressed nicely, but had a big bag that didn't quite belong with her outfit.

She said, "It's okay. Just didn't expect to see a..."

She paused a beat and said, "Man standing there."

My first thought was that she was going to say: *giant*. I was used to scaring people.

I said, "Again, I'm sorry, ma'am. I'm looking for my friend. Did you see her in there?"

She laughed and said, "Young man, there's no one in there. There's barely room for me in there."

I tilted to one side, and looked behind her, inspected the women's bathroom. It was a small room. It was smaller than the men's by almost half.

I guessed that because they didn't have a urinal, the designer of the bar figured it didn't need to be as big.

"Did you see her maybe when you went in?"

She shook her head, said, "No one was here when I went in."

"Thanks."

I turned and looked back at the bar. Talbern wasn't there.

She hadn't walked past me.

Did she ditch me?

I reached into my pocket and pulled out the card that I had paid with. It had her name on it. Plain as day.

No way would she have ditched me and left her card.

22

I WALKED out of the martini bar. I passed the hostess and went through the front door. A couple were locked in an embrace, like they hadn't seen each other in years.

The street was busy with hurried pedestrians and honking taxi cabs and people standing around waiting for Ubers, and a group of people who had left the lounge to smoke cigarettes on the street corner.

No cars were parked out front except for drop-offs.

I frowned.

I took a left and walked back the way we had come. I walked to the street corner and looked left, looked right. I saw no sign of Talbern.

I crossed the street. I didn't want to deviate because, eventually, she'd head back to the hotel.

Once I crossed the street, I walked past another bar and then an all-night convenience store.

Around the side of the building, I came to a service alley.

I looked left. A black sedan was parked in the center of the alley. The engine hummed. Exhaust pooled at the rear of the car. A driver sat on the front bench behind the wheel. I couldn't see his eyes, but he sure was staring at me from the rearview mirror.

He looked like a personal driver. The sedan was a polished and well-kept ride. It was also unmarked. I couldn't tell whether it was some sort of town car or a full-size vehicle. I couldn't tell the make or model.

There was someone in the backseat, a woman. She was talking to him; I guessed by her movements. She seemed upset with him, like he had gotten lost, and she wasn't happy about it.

That's when I realized the driver was the Secret Service agent from the lounge or another member of the same team. He had that earpiece curling out of his ear and disappearing down into his shirt.

Suddenly, there was someone standing directly behind me. I didn't even hear him approach until he was right there.

I turned, and there was a tall man, tall as me. He had a handsome face. Clean-shaven and slicked-back hair, but not wet looking. His eyes were deep set. The color was a mystery to me in the alley's darkness because they were too deep set to see them.

He said, "Mr. Widow?"

I nodded.

He said, "The United States Secret Service would like to have a word with you."

23

"Where's Agent Talbern?" I asked.

"Don't worry. That's her right there. In the car."

I nodded, said, "You snatched her as she left the bathroom?"

"No. Nothing like that. She's an officer of the law. We don't harass fellow federal agents."

"She just got in the car on her own?"

"Yes. We had someone call her. And then we explained the situation. She got in on her own."

"What is this about?"

"Would you get in the car?"

I glanced down at his clothes. He was also dressed like a Secret Service agent, same as the guy I saw in the lounge, but he wasn't the guy. That guy must've been the driver.

I wasn't looking him over for his choice in clothing. I was looking for a gun which he had.

Pulled tight under his jacket was a shoulder rig. It was nearly invisible under his jacket. It was the gun that gave it away.

I turned to look at the car, then back at him.

I said, "Sure. You lead the way."

He nodded and walked past me.

I followed.

He opened the back door for me. I got in next to Talbern.

"You okay?"

She looked unharmed, but she was obviously upset.

She said, "Yes, but what the hell is going on?!"

She was directing the question at me, but her anger at the driver.

"I think we're about to find out."

The other guy closed my door, stepped forward, and got into the passenger seat.

He looked at the driver and said, "Let's go."

The driver nodded and put the car into drive and eased forward.

Talbern said, "Where the hell are we going?"

No answer.

I leaned over to Talbern and asked, "You sure these guys are Secret Service?"

She looked at me and said, "I got a direct call from the office of the FBI director. He vouched for them."

She said it so they could hear her. They didn't respond.

At the end of the alleyway, the driver stopped and looked both ways. Then he headed out into traffic.

The agent in the passenger seat turned back and looked at us.

He said, "My name is Clayton. This is Special Agent Daniels."

I said nothing.

"I'm a former Secret Service agent. Mr. Daniels is the current one. We work for a very important man. I'd like to ask both of you to come with us."

I looked at Talbern. She kept her hands down, resting on

her lap. I checked up on her torso to make sure that she still had her gun. She did.

She said, "Why?"

"It's better if Mr. Widow hears this from my employer."

"You went over my SAC's head. So what choice do we have?"

Clayton said, "Mr. Widow has a choice. You're not prisoners. This is simply a favor from one agency to another."

Clayton looked at me.

"What do you say, Widow?"

"Like the woman said. What choice I got?"

Clayton smiled.

He said, "My boss will explain everything once we get there."

* * *

WE DROVE FOR NEARLY AN HOUR, and we didn't get very far before I worried because we were driving to JFK.

That's when Talbern asked, "Where the hell are we going?"

No answer.

She said, "We're not getting on a plane."

"Don't worry. You won't be," Clayton said.

Talbern's face looked confused, which must've matched my own.

For the second time in twenty-four hours, I was passing through an unmarked security gate with Talbern, headed into an airport. Only this time, the security guards gave us even less fuss than the last time. Secret Service has priority over the FBI, I guessed.

We drove down a long service road, then we turned right and followed along an unused runway.

I looked out the window and saw a distant runway light up. I watched as a plane came in and landed.

The memories of seeing a thousand fighter jets land on battle carriers came flashing across my mind.

Seeing the commercial jet land didn't even compare.

The driver slowed the car and took a soft right. He slowed the car to a stop in front of a private hangar. And suddenly I realized why Clayton had said that we weren't getting on a plane.

Parked in front of the hangar was a blue Agusta AW139 helicopter, which is a big luxury helicopter.

Out front were three more Secret Service agents and a pilot.

The pilot stuck out like a sore thumb. He was a pudgy, short guy, dressed like he was going golfing. He wore a red polo shirt and white golf shorts. Instead of golf shoes, he wore boat shoes. No socks.

The agents all wore the same professional attire. Dark suits. Clip-on ties. And earpieces. All were clean-shaven.

They stood in formation in front of the helicopter. I guessed this was a rehearsed protection stance straight out of the Secret Service playbook.

We pulled up and circled around, and the driver parked the car.

Clayton said, "Let's go."

He opened the door for me. The driver stayed in the car, and Talbern followed out my side instead of trying to open her door.

Clayton walked over to the pilot and asked, "What are you waiting for? Get it going!"

The pilot jumped to it and got in the cockpit, pressed buttons and flipped switches.

The Agusta's engine bustled to life, and the main rotors spun and whirred. The rear rotor rolled and followed suit.

Clayton turned to his men and barked at them to get onboard. Then he turned to us and gestured for us to follow him.

We boarded the helicopter. Two of the agents sat on either side of us. Clayton sat across from us, back to the cockpit. The leftover agent sat in the front, next to the pilot.

The interior of the helicopter reminded me of Marine One. It was decked out with white leather seats and wooden tabletop consoles.

We waited there for another minute while the driver parked the car and came up and hopped in, sitting next to Clayton.

The pilot wore a headset. He reached back and handed a spare one to Clayton. No one else wore one.

Clayton said, "Let's go."

The pilot acknowledged, and the Agusta roared up into the air. We ascended for several minutes until JFK was a small dot below.

I looked out the window and saw the Atlantic off in the distance.

We headed north on a straight track, toward the unknown.

24

THE AGUSTA AW139 Helicopter flew at a speed slightly faster than steady-going, nothing too dramatic, but fast enough.

We flew over land but traced along the coastline half the way.

Talbern squeezed as close to me as she could, but the console in between us made it impossible for her to get as close as I would've liked.

Clayton didn't make eye contact with me or stare at me, but he seemed always to keep me in his line of sight.

The ride was relatively silent.

Finally, the pilot came on over the headset and said something to Clayton.

Clayton responded, "Okay. Got it."

He looked at Talbern and then me.

He said, "We're landing."

Talbern asked, "Where are we?"

I looked past the guy next to me and saw what looked like the coast of Maine, or possibly New Hampshire.

Even though it was summer, the coastline looked unkind

and harsh and cold at night, not the kind of winter cold that Maine could throw around. But it was a far cry from the Florida summer.

I looked out over the water. It was uninviting and frenetic. Waves violently crashed into the nearby rocks.

The Agusta yawed and tilted and swung around. We lowered. The helicopter tilted enough for me to stare straight at the shoreline.

The pilot took us back above land. We passed over the sharp, jagged rocks. They varied in size. Some were palm-sized rocks, and others were more like broken apart boulders.

We descended onto the back lawn of a sprawling house that was more like a manor than a house.

It was surrounded by a surplus of freshly trimmed hedges and an Olympic lap pool and external lights.

Roman statues lined the walls of the pool. I couldn't see the front of the house, but something told me that there was a fountain.

I saw an impressive two-story greenhouse to the north end of the estate.

The house belonged to someone important. That was clear. And the Secret Service detail meant that someone was a government person. And who has a helicopter pad on in their backyard?

The pilot took us in and slowed over a circle of lights around the helicopter pad. We lowered and hung in the air for a moment and then landed.

Clayton waited until the pilot killed the engine, and the rotors slowed. Then he signaled for his guys to get out. They opened the side doors and hopped out. Talbern and I followed, going out opposite doors. We walked around to the front of the chopper and met in the front.

Talbern ducked her head like she was afraid of the helicopter blades, even though it must've been six feet over her head. I smiled.

Clayton said, "This way."

We followed him. And the three other guys followed us.

I kept glancing at them in the reflection from a pair of double French doors at the rear of the house as we approached.

Clayton opened the doors, and we walked into a big back hallway. There were twenty-foot ceilings, and light fixtures high up, and enormous paintings draped from the walls.

I couldn't name any of them, but I recognized a few.

Mostly they were oil paintings of famous wars, battle-fields, and dead generals.

One was of the battle of Gettysburg. One was of a fictional battle among angels and demons. And one was even of Ulysses S. Grant. It looked like one that he might've sat for.

The lights were set low, like candlelight.

Huge Victorian furniture lined the walls. Old armchairs, tables slid in the corners, displaying fine China and statues of cannons and busts of famous historical people. Many of which I didn't know.

We followed Clayton through more huge double doors. These were big oak things that looked more like they belonged on the outside of a castle with a drawbridge attached, rather than in someone's house.

Talbern said, "Wow! Who lives in a place like this?"

She said it without actually meaning to say it, like a reflex more than an actual question.

Nobody answered her.

Through the doors, we came into a big kitchen. There was a maid. She stood over the stove. She was making tea and possibly doing something else. I wasn't sure what, but I knew she wasn't making coffee.

She turned and waved at us, but didn't speak.

We continued on through a great dining room with a long family table. The places were already set. There were salad bowls stacked neatly on top of dinner plates. There were overturned coffee cups on top of saucers.

The chairs were slid under the tables.

Silverware was set nice and neat.

Everything was clean and polished. However, the whole scene looked barren and unused, like no one lived here, and no one had eaten there in a generation. It was lifeless.

We moved on through a study and then out into a grand foyer.

Clayton looked back at me and motioned for us to keep following. He headed up a hardwood staircase. I stayed a few steps behind with Talbern at my back.

The Secret Service agents were still close behind us.

At the top of the stairs, we turned a corner and walked down a short hallway.

The upstairs was far cozier than the lower level. Everything looked lived in, more like a family dwelling and not a museum.

We passed an open door. I glanced in and saw a good-sized bedroom. The bed was made and didn't look slept in. Then we walked to the last door, which was closed.

Clayton stopped and knocked on it.

A male voice, young and energetic, said, "Come in."

Clayton pushed the door open, and we followed him in.

We walked into a master bedroom that was very lived in.

The room was huge. In one corner, there was a grand piano under a dim spotlight. In the opposite corner, there was a big wall of windows with thick sills big enough to sit on, like a makeshift bench.

There was living room furniture near a far wall. All of it was set up in front of a dormant fireplace.

Family photos lined the walls and tabletops and the mantle above the fireplace. There were photos of kids who were grown into men. There were photos of a husband and wife. And there were more photos of the wife standing alone. All of it seemed to be from a long time ago, another life.

Then there was a desk that looked more Army-issued than it did civilian-bought. The desk was a thick, wooden thing.

A lamp on the desk was clicked on as we entered the room. A young man sat on the edge, staring at us.

On the desk, I saw more photos. Several of them were turned to face outward.

I recognized most of the faces from the photos. There were pictures of two former presidents, a couple of current senators, and several generals. There was even a photo of a group of men, and one of them was the current Russian president.

And then there was one face in all the photos that I only recognized because he was the husband from the family photos. He stood in each of the photos, shaking hands, smiling, and mingling with the famous government officials and army generals.

The last thing in the room was a huge king-size bed. Next to the bed were a couple of expensive hospital machines.

An old, feeble man lay half under the covers of the bed. His torso was up, leaned against a wall of thick body pillows. On the floor, next to the bed, was a pile of extra pillows and a couple of blankets.

The room was cold. I heard Talbern make a *brr* sound under her breath.

The temperature must've been set somewhere in the sixties.

Clayton stopped dead center of the room. He ignored the young guy behind the desk and addressed the old man.

He said, "This is Jack Widow and FBI Agent Talbern."

The old man sat up a little more and looked me up and down. He didn't seem to pay much attention to Talbern.

He said, "Mr. Jack Widow."

Clayton said, "This is Secretary John Dayard."

Talbern gasped like she knew exactly who he was.

Dayard asked, "Do you know who I am?"

He coughed after. Nothing heavy, but enough to get the man at the desk to walk over.

The man must've been a personal nurse because he stepped to the machines and inspected them like he knew what he was doing. Then he tried to offer the secretary a glass of water that was half full, set out on a nightstand.

Dayard waved him away.

He said, "No. No. I'm fine."

He spoke to the nurse with annoyance in his tone, which I had seen before from older people. It was a kind of orneriness.

I said, "You were the secretary of defense for two presidents."

Dayard smiled and said, "I still am. Once you're named secretary of anything, you lose the job duties one day, but you keep the title. So technically, I'm still secretary."

"Are you still a general?"

"That's also a title you keep. Forever."

I stayed quiet.

"Some titles you lose. Like no one ever calls you by your last rank in the military."

"Guess I wasn't good enough."

"Nonsense. You just didn't stay around long enough. Generals aren't guys who get promoted. They're guys who never leave. Stay around something long enough, and they'll just throw medals and titles at you."

I nodded.

Dayard coughed again and waved off the nurse before he could react.

He said, "Leave us."

The nurse nodded like a loyal subject would have a thousand years ago. And he left the room.

Dayard said, "You too."

He was talking to Clayton.

Clayton didn't nod or say a word. He simply turned and left the room. He closed the door on the way out, leaving the three of us alone.

I heard the summer wind rapping against the glass outside the window. Then I heard it whistle from out of the fireplace like a gust of wind was trapped down the shoot.

Dayard noticed it and said, "There are cracks in the brick. Sometimes the whole thing whistles like a giant flute."

"You should get it plugged up," I said.

He said nothing to that.

Talbern spoke for the first time since we came into the room. She walked past me and closer to the center of the room, where Clayton had been standing.

She asked, "Mr. Dayard, what are we doing here, sir?"

"Straight to the point. I like that. The reason you're both here is because of Widow."

Talbern looked at me.

"I know about the new missing girl."

He said it, seemingly without concern.

Talbern asked, "How do you know about that?"

"I'm an old has-been. But I still have connections."

"What do you want?"

But Dayard didn't answer that. Instead, he pulled himself

up. He removed the covers. He was dressed in pajamas that looked more like his wife had picked them out for him rather than he purchased them for himself.

They were black and silk with blue piping.

He put one foot down on the carpet and then the other. He stood up fine and pulled off the tubes that were suction cupped to his arm. A heart monitor machine beeped. He reached over and switched it off.

"Shut up," he said to it.

He could stand okay but looked even feebler than he had before, lying in bed. He was about the frailest person I ever saw. He was scrawny and looked malnourished.

He walked over to the fireplace, slowly and sluggishly.

He sat on one of the heavy armchairs and said, "Sit. Both of you."

We sat on a sofa—Talbern to my right, closer to the fireplace.

Dayard reached out and picked up a family photo off a coffee table. He stared at it for a long, long moment. He appeared to be lost in some long-dead memory.

Finally, he asked, "You got a family?"

I said, "I had one."

He nodded and said, "Your mother."

I stayed quiet. He had already known. I assumed he knew far more about me than I did him.

"She was murdered, right?"

I nodded.

"You used to be an undercover cop?"

Talbern looked at me. I guess she didn't know that part about me.

I said, "I was. NCIS. But you already knew that."

"That's why you're here."

I waited, said nothing.

"I had a family once too. I had a wife and two sons."

Dayard turned the photo toward us and reached it out, long. He gestured for me to take it.

I did.

"Look."

I looked. It was a photo of a young family. Dayard was there, holding hands with a woman, and there were two young boys.

He said, "My sons. James and John, Jr. That was my second wife. Not their mother. She died in childbirth to James."

"Good-looking family," I said, with no idea of what I was supposed to say.

"They were. They were."

He reached out to take the photo back. I handed it over to him.

"My wife and son are dead now."

Talbern said, "I'm sorry."

I stayed quiet.

"My wife died giving birth to James, our youngest."

He paused a somber beat and said, "John killed himself. Years ago."

He looked at the empty fireplace and said, "Widow, you from a military family, right? Mother was a Marine?"

I said, "Yes."

"What about your father? I saw nothing about him in your records."

"Don't know him, sir."

"Not at all?"

"Never met him. He was a nobody. A drifter."

"Is that why you live how you live now? Trying to find him?"

"Maybe."

"Military families are hard to grow up in. My first-born son, John, felt that pressure. Once, we were a happy family. Even though they lost their mother, my sons were good boys. I was hard on them. Too hard.

"John wanted so badly to follow in my footsteps. He wanted to impress me. He joined the Army. Like I did.

"Then he was booted out. He couldn't make it through boot camp. They said he had psychological problems. That nearly crushed him."

Silence fell between us.

Talbern said, "Mr. Secretary..."

But he interrupted her.

"Just let me finish."

She nodded.

"My oldest son, John, Jr., couldn't handle the shame of disappointing me. He couldn't handle how it looked for him to have been booted out of the Army."

He took in a deep breath and said, "It's my fault."

I asked, "What is?"

Dayard said, "My oldest son killed himself."

25

DAYARD STARED into the fireplace like there was a roaring fire in it. Like a man lost in thought. Like he was acting out a scene that had been blocked and directed for a play.

Talbern said, "Forgive me, sir. But we're aware of what happened to your oldest son."

"Did Widow know?"

I shook my head.

"My son, John, didn't kill himself right off. He was thrown out of the Army. He moved home and bounced around from job to job. We ignored his problems. We pretended everything was fine, at first.

"My next son made it into the Army. At first, John seemed happy for him. Like he was proud of his younger brother, but that all changed quickly because James rose through the ranks. He was promoted fast.

"John stayed up in his room. He stopped coming down during the daytime."

I waited and listened. I knew there was more to tell. But Dayard didn't add more. He stayed quiet. His eyes teared up a bit.

Finally, I asked, "What happened next?"

"John was very jealous that his brother had been successful. It's partially my fault. I shouldn't have made my disappointment in him so obvious.

"It all happened when his brother got accepted to officer school. I think that was the straw that broke his back."

"What did he do?" I asked.

"John took our family boat out. He took it out alone. He took it out into the Gulf of Maine. Deep."

He turned and looked at me. His eyes were emotional. They looked genuinely sad.

He said, "He jumped into the water and drowned himself."

I paused a beat, and then I asked, "How do you know it was intentional?"

"He radioed the Coast Guard. There's a tape."

"He told them what he was going to do?"

Dayard nodded, said, "He said that he wanted us to find the boat. He didn't want me to think that it had been stolen."

Silence fell over the room.

Dayard fidgeted his fingers and then moved his hand across the top of his pajamas. He felt around a breast pocket that was empty, like he was looking for cigarettes.

He didn't find any.

I was sure that he did this out of habit more than anything else. The nurse probably was constantly taking them away from him. Or maybe not.

Dayard said, "They played the recording in court. At my other son's trial."

"Why did they do that? Talbern asked.

"The prosecution thought that it would show James was disturbed. They wanted to show that psychotic tendencies ran in my family. All a part of the evidence against him."

"The defense allowed that?"

"They believed it might help James's case. Like the traumatic loss of killing his mother in childbirth and then his brother committing suicide had traumatized him so much that he started killing those women."

Dayard paused for a moment, and then he said, "It was all crap!"

Talbern said, "Mr. Secretary, the FBI already knows all of this."

He didn't respond.

She said, "Why are we here?"

He seemed to get upset. His gray eyebrows furrowed, and he turned a shade of red, like he was boiling over.

But he maintained a calm voice. He said, "You found another body?"

Talbern looked confused and said, "No, sir."

Then Dayard looked confused. He asked, "Then, why is your agency reopening the case?"

"We're not," Talbern lied.

Dayard looked at me for an answer. But my face remained the same.

"Agent Talbern, I know your agency has renewed interest."

Silence.

"For God's sake! My son will be executed in two days! You can save his life!"

Talbern was gripping my arm. Her nails were cut short, but they still dug into my skin.

Dayard took a breath and paused a moment. Then he said, "I know you found something. Now, I don't know what."

He stopped at the "what" like he was giving Talbern a moment to respond. A notable tactic used in undercover interrogation, also known as subtle interrogation.

When a cop is undercover, it is impossible to interrogate assets traditionally. So typically, subtle interrogation tactics are employed. Lead someone in a conversation. Make them feel a part of it. You say this and that. Leave off information that they know, and nine times out of ten, they'll volunteer it.

Talbern gave nothing away.

She stayed silent.

Dayard said, "Whatever you have found can at least get him a stay of execution."

"All I can tell you, sir, is that the FBI will do everything that it can to follow the law and make sure that justice is done."

Dayard rested the palms of his hands on the armrests of the chair. He stretched his fingers out.

He nodded and said, "The official position."

We said nothing.

He looked away for a long moment. This was another scene that felt rehearsed. There was something almost cinematic about him.

The guy had a presence, even if he was a shell of the two-star general I imagined he used to be.

He turned back to us and asked, "Talbern, will you excuse us for a moment?"

She stayed where she was, and then she said, "Yes."

Talbern looked at me, nodded, and then she got up and left the room.

"Widow, can I be honest with you?"

"I hope so, sir."

"I saw your records."

"Seems like everyone is doing that tonight."

"Your records are the reason that I know you found a new dog tag."

I stayed quiet.

"The FBI ran your Navy records. As you know, some of your records are classified beyond classified."

I nodded.

"That set off some red flags. Obviously."

"You're not in the Navy, General."

"No. I'm not. But the Navy answers to the same department as the Army and the Air Force and the Marine Corps."

I sat back on the sofa, crossed my foot over my knee.

"The DOD."

"The Department of Defense," he said, nodding. "Know who is in charge of the DOD?"

"The current secretary of defense."

"The current secretary was on my team, way back when I was in charge. He owes me. And he knew my son."

"He called you."

"He called me."

"He told you about the dog tags."

"No. Actually, he referred me to the MPs in Graham, down in Florida. I called there, personally, and spoke to a guy named Hamilton. He told me. The FBI doesn't work for me, but the Army sure as hell used to."

Silence. I noticed the tears in his eyes had dried up, and now he was showing me the face of a former general. Some remnants of the face he used to show his officers when he was barking orders at them. I was certain.

"You're not in the Army, but you were a sailor for fifteen years."

"Sixteen, but only four. Technically." I said. "I was in the NCIS for thirteen. I wasn't technically in the military anymore. I was a civilian."

"That's sixteen years that you were deployed with military men. As far as I'm concerned, you're one of us. You were a SEAL. That's even more one of us."

I nodded. He wasn't wrong about that point.

I said, "Look, I'm just a guy now. I don't work for the military anymore."

"Aren't you helping the FBI?"

"Yeah, but that's against my will."

"They're forcing you?"

"They were using handcuffs."

He said, "Isn't the Navy SEAL slogan 'All in, all the time'? Something like that?"

I nodded and said, "We've got a lot of slogans. Another is 'Don't run to your death.'"

"I need your help."

I sat there.

"If you found another dog tag, then another girl has been killed."

I looked away from him and glanced around the room again.

Dayard grabbed the photo of his family again. He showed it to me again.

"Look at them!"

I looked.

"James is the only one left. I've got cancer, Widow."

"I'm sorry," I said, with nothing else really to say.

"It's bad. I won't live through the year. My son is the only person left in my family.

"Widow, he's innocent. I know he is!"

"What do you want me to do?"

"The FBI thinks he's guilty. They think he killed one of their own during a raid."

"I was told that."

"They will not pursue this. They don't care if he dies. They want it all shut down. Case closed."

Dayard took another deep breath and coughed briefly, and then he asked, "Did you look over the case files?"

"I saw what they gave me."

"Looking at your records, you were a brilliant investigator. What did you see?"

"I was an undercover operative. I didn't investigate crimes in the traditional way. You need to trust the FBI on this."

"What did you see?"

I paused for a moment and wondered if I should tell him anything about it. Was I allowed to share information? Then I thought he probably already knew most of it because there had been a trial.

"I saw the bodies. Read about the women."

"All the murders were the same?"

"Not the same. Nothing is ever the same. But close enough."

"Same murderer?"

"That part is obvious. Has to be."

"Why do you think so?"

"The dog tag. That the women were all AWOL."

"And that none of that stuff was reported?"

I half nodded and said, "The AWOL part was written about before the trial."

"But the FBI never released that information. It was put together by the media."

I shrugged.

"What I'm asking is, don't you agree that the killer of these women is all the same man?"

I shrugged.

"What kind of chance is there that a random killer, a stranger to the real killer, would duplicate the dog tags? How would anyone know about that?"

"People talk."

"That's not likely. The juror was under orders by the judge. Even after they leave trial, they can't reveal that information."

"You can't police that."

"Don't you think my son deserves a second look? If you found a new dog tag, then he should get the stay of execution."

I said nothing.

"Just do this, old man a favor. Look into it for me. Look at how they got to him."

I stared at Dayard's face, hard. He was genuine, but any father would be.

Then I looked down at the coffee table, thought for a moment.

How did they catch Dayard?

I thought back to the files that I read. They tracked the bodies being dumped out of the old harbor in Portland. It used to be the main port after the American Revolution.

Times change. Cities grow. Needs change. Now, there was a huge port and various boat harbors all over the place.

I closed my eyes and recalled the text in my head.

Marksy and Lowe had gotten to Dayard's boat. This was a part of their investigation that I liked. They were desperate for a crack in the case. So, they reached out to the US Coast Guard, who referred them to the US Navy.

The Navy used good old-fashioned seaway patterning to search for a pattern for the dumping of the bodies; only the "old-fashioned" part was mixed with drones. They narrowed the seaways down to Portland, which led to nothing because Portland had thousands of boats and ships, corporate and private.

But they cross-referenced the passages of boats around a stretch of waterway called the Chickadee Pass.

They narrowed the killer's routes down to this pass because it was an area that was both hardly traveled, giving the killer privacy, and it was at the apex of the dumping patterns. It made sense to rank it high on the list of pattern searches.

Two things stuck out to Marksy and Lowe and the sailors, helping them. The first was that they were positive the killer was passing through Chickadee Pass. The odds were almost certain of it.

The second thing was that the year they caught the killer, the Maine State Congress had passed a bill protecting the Chickadee Pass from divers, fishermen, and even boats from passing through it.

The Chickadee Pass was a tiny area of water, several miles from the coastline, north of Portland. It got its name because there was a little uninhabited island that was a major migration outpost for the black-capped chickadee.

The black-capped chickadee is Maine's official state bird.

The island was declared a protected habitat of the bird. That led to the Coast Guard monitoring the area with drones that would fly over at least once a day.

As luck would have it, they spotted the Dayard family boat passing through a few times, enough to parallel it with the discovery of a body.

Marksy and Lowe didn't want to wait on surveillance because there was a woman missing.

This wasn't in the report. But I imagined they wanted to save her life. Catching a murderer and saving one victim all in one raid was a prize for law enforcement. So rarely did we ever get to see both the look on a rescued victim's face and the total disappointment on a criminal's face before he's read his rights.

I knew the desire to feeling this. I had that feeling.

That's how they discovered the Dayard boat. They tracked it to an old dock among hundreds of boats.

They raided it. Lowe was shot.

The killer got away.

I opened my eyes. Beyond that, I knew no more details about that night.

The report had no more detail.

Secretary Dayard stared at me with hope in his eyes.

"Please, Widow, help us."

Don't run to your death.

I nodded and said, "I'll do what I can."

"Thank you! Thank you!"

I stood up, stretched my legs.

Dayard also stood up.

He reached his hand out to shake mine. I took it and shook it. The whole thing felt like a gentleman's deal, like a pledge.

I walked out of the room, left him in the doorway.

Dayard spoke to Clayton alone. I met Talbern downstairs.

"What did he say?"

"What do you think?"

"He wants you to prove his son is innocent in less than two days?"

I asked, "What time is it?"

Talbern took out her cellphone. She unlocked it with a passcode and ignored a text from Kelvin, as well as several missed calls from him.

She noticed I noticed, and she said, "I texted him what was going on. When they first asked me to get in the car."

I nodded.

"It's almost two-thirty."

"We'd better get back."

"Are you going to help?"

"I already told Pawn I would."

"Yeah, but that was to help us find Karen Dekker. What about Dayard? You going to help him too?"

"I don't care about him. He's had a long life. I only want to find this girl alive. Let's save her life. If we can prove along the way that his kid is innocent, then great."

"We need to get back."

"I need some sleep."

She said, "So do I."

After a couple of minutes, Clayton came down and said, "Come with me."

We followed him back through the huge house and to the Agusta AW139 helicopter. The pilot was already in the cockpit. The rotor blades started spinning when he saw us exit the manor.

We flew back to New York. This time. It was just Clayton, me and Talbern, and the pilot.

The same driver from earlier waited for us at JFK.

Clayton walked us to the car. He didn't get in. He waited for me and said, "I got to get back. But here's my card. That's my personal cellphone. Call me anytime. This is very important to Secretary Dayard."

I looked at the card and then at the shadows that covered his eyes.

"This says retired Secret Service?"

"I'm not with the Service anymore. Just head of Dayard's security."

"Are all of your guys retired?"

"We're all private. Technically. Dayard isn't in public life anymore. Therefore, he doesn't get Secret Service protection."

"You guys all look the part."

"We all were. Every man that works with me, I hand-selected."

"Why so many guards?"

He stopped, looked at the top of the car, said, "Dayard had a long career. He made some enemies. Plus, the whole thing with his son has brought some hate mail and such. Why?"

"If his son is innocent, then I have to look at every possibility."

He nodded and rapped on the trunk lid of the car, signaling to the driver to head out.

"You have a good night. Thanks for helping us out."

I nodded and got into the car. We drove away from the airport. We sat in silence the whole way back to the hotel, but Talbern sat close to me.

At the hotel, we got out of the car. We didn't say a word to the driver. We went up to my room.

Talbern came in, which I wasn't expecting. She sat down on the bed.

"What did Kelvin say?"

"I didn't tell him yet. Just told him we were approached by the Secret Service."

"They weren't Secret Service."

"What?"

"Not technically. Clayton told me all those guys are former agents. Now, they're private."

"He showed me a badge!"

"It's probably real. Probably never turned it back in whenever he left the Service."

"They have to!"

"No. They're *supposed* to. Not the same. It doesn't matter, anyway. They would've gotten us to speak with them no matter what. Dayard has a lot of connections."

"So he mentioned. Did you know him before tonight?"

"I heard of him. He reached the rank of two-star. He was

from the Armored Division. He had a solid reputation. Best, I knew."

I yawned, which I hadn't meant to. But Talbern saw it.

She said, "We should get some sleep."

I paused a moment because part of me hoped she meant together, but I knew that was a stupid thought.

I nodded.

"What's the next step?" I asked.

"Tomorrow, we should check in with Pawn, and then I guess brief with Marksy. Maybe we should go see Dayard. The son."

"What for?"

"Don't you think you should meet with him? See what you think of him?"

"Not sure. I'm not buying he's this innocent pawn who got arrested by mistake. Marksy's notes are pretty thorough. She seems like a good agent."

"What about the killer murdering her husband?"

"What about it?" I asked.

"Makes for an interesting argument why she might be blinded to the facts of the case."

"Maybe. But Pawn said there was an entire task force involved. They wouldn't have just let her go rogue. Blame some sucker for the whole thing."

I paused another long beat.

"What is it?"

"I didn't read why they picked Dayard."

"You didn't read the whole thing about how they connected the boat? It was because of a bird."

"I read that part. I mean. That night they tried to raid the boat. It's presumed that the killer was onboard. He shot Lowe and got away. But they never saw his face."

"Right."

"So how does Marksy know it was him?"

"She saw him. It says that in the report."

"It does? I missed that part. But is that all?"

She asked, "What more do you need?"

"I don't believe that Pawn would've gone to arrest the son of a decorated and influential former secretary of defense on just her eyewitness testimony."

"She's a federal agent."

"I know. But she also just saw her husband get shot."

Talbern said, "They didn't just go on her account. There's another witness who connected Dayard to one of the girls."

"Another witness? I didn't read about that?"

"Did you even read any of the report?"

"Most of it."

"Details, Jack. Details are important."

I yawned again. This time I covered my mouth because I saw it coming.

I spoke in a yawning voice.

"I should get to bed. In the morning, we'll go see Marksy. You can tell me about the witness tomorrow."

She nodded and stood up from the bed. She walked casually by me. Talbern had quite a strut. She had soft features in the front, but hard in the back. Like she was a woman who tried to look like a woman, but still maintained her muscle tone for work in a man's profession.

My mother taught me to be a gentleman, a southern thing. But she didn't teach me to be a monk. And monks are celibate, not gentlemen. So, I did as any man would do when a woman like Talbern walks past him.

I watched.

She stopped at the door, turned back to me, and said, "Get some sleep, Jack."

No one ever called me Jack. I preferred to be called Widow, but I didn't correct her. I liked the way she said it.

"Good night."

She walked out, and I kicked my shoes off, crashed on the bed.

26

I SLEPT a few hours before I woke straight up and stared at the ceiling.

Everything in the Hotel George was top-notch. Even the ceilings had crown molding. The FBI treated its guests like VIP. Then again, they arrested me and flew me against my will over nine states.

I wasn't too mad about it. The way I lived my life was literally going with the flow. But sometimes, there were things that called for me to go against the flow, to swim upriver.

Potentially I was looking at an innocent man on death row who was about to be executed. I was looking at a missing woman who might still be alive. And I was looking at a serial killer who was getting away with it.

I woke up because I couldn't sleep any longer. I kept thinking of Karen Dekker.

What if the real AWOL killer was still out there? What if he had Dekker?

If she was still alive, I wanted to find her before it was too late.

I thought about the killer.

The FBI report stated that the AWOL case was closed over a year ago. Calculating the length of the trial and the last victim found, I would estimate that AWOL hadn't killed in twenty-two months, almost two years.

Why would he kill that time?

Why did he move to Florida?

If this was a real AWOL murder case, then I could guess that the reason he stopped was that he knew that they had captured someone else. He saw an opportunity for the FBI to pin the whole thing on James Dayard.

I'm sure he wanted to throw the FBI off his trail.

Maybe he never stopped. Maybe he simply adjusted his targets or moved to another country.

I recalled a theory about the infamous serial killer called the Zodiac. Some so-called scholars proclaimed a theory where the real killer was diagnosed with cancer, and he moved to Mexico to live out his days with cancer therapies. DNA was just coming up, and the guy didn't want his DNA to be on file somewhere in the US.

I didn't know about any of that, but I knew from living a life of going with the flow that shit happens.

Maybe shit happened to AWOL. And he stopped for a while.

Next to the bed, on a nightstand, was a lamp, a slick portable phone, and an alarm clock. The clock was digital with soft-lighted numbers.

The time was seven in the morning.

I groaned, looking at it, and turned over to look at the open doorway to the bathroom.

I closed my eyes again.

* * *

I SLEPT ALMOST two hours before waking up at ten past nine in the morning. I got out of bed, showered, and got back into my own clothes. I folded Kelvin's up neat and made the hotel bed. I left the clothes there, took the tablet that Pawn had given me, and went down to the lobby.

There wasn't a restaurant, but there was a complimentary breakfast station set up. There were only two other people there, both older than me, by twenty years, and both were male, and both sat separately, reading newspapers.

I didn't see the employee who set up the station anywhere in sight.

I looked over everything. It was the most disappointing thing about the hotel. It was all pretty standard American breakfast foods, minus eggs and bacon, which was what I was hoping for. Instead, there was nothing but on-the-go foods, like cereal and doughnuts and bagels.

I grabbed a blueberry bagel and a cup of coffee.

The bagel was pretty good. I ended up eating two of them and drinking four cups of the coffee because the cups were small to-go things and not those bucket-sizes that Starbucks serves.

To be honest, I wasn't sure which I liked better because I grew up seeing the value of good things coming in small packages. But then again, I was a big guy, and I liked coffee. More seemed better to me than less.

I sat at a table alone and looked over the rest of the case reports on the tablet.

I finally found the so-called witness. It was the husband of the victim that Dayard had been linked to. Her name was Becci Scarpone.

Her husband said that he saw Dayard hanging around their home after she had broken the whole thing off.

The husband claimed Dayard was texting, calling her for

weeks. He said that in her final days; she seemed scared to go anywhere until one day she vanished.

I sat back and turned off the tablet. I wouldn't get any more from reading it.

The witness they used was the former husband of one victim, and a man cheated on. I could see a strong defense, at least being able to say his testimony was circumstantial.

He didn't see Dayard kill his wife. All his testimony did was paint a very bad picture of James Dayard.

I imagined that his testimony, combined with Marksy's and the notes of a dead FBI agent, was enough to seal Dayard's fate.

Just then, Talbern and Kelvin appeared from the elevators.

Talbern smiled at me. She looked a lot more rested than I did. I was sure of that.

Kelvin didn't smile, but he nodded. He was wearing the same clothes as yesterday. I had his spares, after all.

Kelvin went to look at the breakfast food, and Talbern came right to me. She sat down.

I said, "Aren't you going to get some coffee?"

And just then, she showed me the first thing about her that turned me off.

"I don't drink coffee."

"What?" I said. I couldn't see my own expression, but I was sure I had a genuine shock on my face.

She smiled hard and asked, "Does that offend you?"

"No. Not at all. Just surprising."

"Why's that?"

"I just never met a cop who didn't like coffee."

"I didn't say that I don't like it."

"Why don't you have some then?"

"I'm allergic."

"Say what?"

"I'm allergic to caffeine."

I stayed quiet.

"It's a rare thing, but it happens. So I don't drink soda, coffee, or energy drinks. I can't even have tea. It sucks."

"You've never had coffee?"

"Nope. Never," she said, then she thought for a moment and said, "Well one time. That's how we found out."

"That's just about the worse thing I've ever heard in my life."

She shrugged and said, "It's not that bad. At least I'll keep my youthful skin."

"Not sure if coffee causes premature aging. Think that's just something that tea makers want us to think so they can sell more tea."

"Maybe. At any rate, I can't have it."

I said, "They got juice."

"Kelvin's grabbing me some."

I nodded, took another pull of my coffee.

"Did you tell him about last night?"

She nodded.

"What did he say?"

"He was shocked about it, but said little."

"We should speak to Marksy and this witness too."

"Okay. We'll see her at the office."

I nodded.

Just then, Kelvin's cellphone rang. He put down a plate with a doughnut on it and answered the phone.

Talbern looked over at him. She watched his face like she knew all of his expressions enough to get the gist of the conversation.

He talked for a moment and then clicked off. He left his doughnut and walked over to us.

"We gotta go."

Talbern asked, "What's going on?"

"They found her."

"Dekker?" I asked.

He nodded.

"Is she alive?" Talbern asked, but I already knew the answer from Kelvin's demeanor, and I guessed Talbern did too. But she asked out of concern and reflex.

"No. She's dead."

27

BEFORE I KNEW IT, we were back at JFK Airport. Same private hangar area, the same plane that the FBI had flown me in on coming from Florida.

The flight crew was different this time around. Instead of the guy from yesterday, we had a female flight attendant and a female pilot with a male co-pilot.

The flight attendant went through all the same motions, saying hello to us as we boarded the plane.

Everything was basically the same as the flight to New York from Florida. Except for this time, I wasn't in restraints, and the crew was different, and Marksy was waiting onboard to greet us.

Despite the news that Dekker was found dead, she was more polite to me than the day before.

I sat at a window seat, and Talbern sat next to me.

Marksy got up and moved to our row.

Before the pilot taxied to the runway for takeoff, Marksy said, "Widow, I'm sorry for the way I behaved to you."

That was big of her, I thought.

"Don't worry about it."

"You know what it's like having someone show up out of the blue with evidence that reopens your case?"

"I don't, actually. But I can imagine."

"It throws a monkey wrench into everything."

I stayed quiet.

"Did you look over the case?" she asked.

"Yeah."

"Then, you can understand my position?"

"Of course."

She paused briefly.

She said, "It's been twenty-two months and thirteen days since he killed him."

Her voice was part emotion and part professional FBI, in that Eliot Ness sort of way. She sounded like a tax accountant with a very matter-of-fact sort of tone.

I nodded.

"Dayard's guilty. I know it. He shot my husband. And murdered those women."

I said nothing.

"I'm not sure who's doing this. But he killed those others."

She said it with more than conviction. She said it as if she was certain of it. It was true, no matter what, which was a dangerous thing.

A cop who *knows* a perp is guilty, even though the evidence wasn't one hundred percent, was a cop who had a grudge.

Marksy had every right to have a grudge. I understood one hundred percent. No question. But her grudge was against the man who killed her husband, and that man wasn't necessarily the man they arrested for it.

I said nothing else about it. Just repeated, "Don't worry about it."

The airplane finished taxiing to the runway. We sat back and waited.

The engines bellowed, and the plane shotgunned toward the sky.

28

WE LANDED BACK at the same airport in Orlando and took the same SUV back to Graham.

Going through the gate, I had the feeling that I would see Coresca working the gate. Of course he was.

Kelvin drove us. When he pulled up to the gate, the first thing that Coresca did was to ask to see Kelvin's ID. Then he recognized him. He looked at Marksy, who was in the passenger seat. Then he looked back to see Talbern and me.

His eyes locked on me.

In one second, he had his hand out, waiting for Kelvin to hand over his ID. The next, he stepped back and reached for what I thought was his gun, like he was suspicious that somehow I had escaped FBI custody and taken these agents hostage and forced them to return me to Graham base. Maybe he thought it was to return to murder him for treating me like crap when I was here.

To tell the truth, I wasn't happy to see him. But I was happy for him to see me returning, not in handcuffs, but as a temporary consultant to the FBI.

He continued to stare and reach for something that was out of my view.

I stared back at him. I smiled, but didn't react otherwise.

Of course, he didn't draw his gun.

He pulled up a radio. He clicked the button and asked for Hamilton to respond. He didn't use any radio codes.

"Go ahead," Hamilton's voice said.

Coresca said, "They're here."

"The FBI?"

"Yes. And they brought him back."

"Good. Send them through."

Coresca paused a long, long beat, like he was pondering how much time in prison an Army tribunal would give him if he shot me dead.

Hamilton asked, "Coresca?"

"Ten-four," he said, and placed the radio back down on his belt.

He said nothing to me. He turned back to the gate. We waited for a long minute, and finally, Marksy asked, "What the hell is his problem?"

Kelvin reached up and adjusted the rearview, looked at me.

Talbern didn't budge.

Marksy sensed something was amiss with them. She looked at me.

I shrugged and said, "Think that guy's got a brain problem."

"I guess so."

"Maybe he was dropped on his head as a kid," Talbern added.

I smiled.

"Guess so," Marksy said.

Coresca returned with a tag to hang from the rearview mirror. He handed it to Kelvin and then pointed north.

"Head straight. The medical building is a two-story building on the end."

Kelvin nodded and drove forward, stopping at the gate for Coresca to open it.

We passed through and drove straight. Kelvin performed a couple of California stops at two intersections.

He pulled into a parking lot behind the medical building and parked near the front.

We got out and walked up a hill to a sidewalk. There were no stairs. We walked right in.

A female sergeant behind a desk greeted us and escorted us through a set of double doors and down a short hallway. We stopped and went through an unmarked door with chipped, green paint.

On the other side, she stopped at another desk in a small office.

A wiry guy sat behind it. He didn't wear an army uniform. He was in green scrubs. This meant that he was a doctor, but I didn't know what kind.

In the military, there is the Medical Corps, so most doctors are designated a certain title such as: *flight surgeon*. I wasn't sure what his would've been. In the civilian world, he was simply a coroner.

Since Graham was such a small base, I was sure he probably was some sort of general practitioner. Maybe the only MD on post, which explained his tired look.

He looked like he hadn't slept in days. He was drinking a cup of coffee, which I immediately noticed, but didn't ask for any.

He stood up and asked, "Is this them?"

"Yes, sir."

"Dismissed, Sergeant," he said.

The desk sergeant turned and smiled at me with something behind the smile, like she knew who I was and the whole story about Coresca and my getting detained.

She walked out of the room.

The guy said, "I'm Dr. Shpoik."

It sounded a lot like Spock from the Star Trek TV show. Obviously, he knew that because he wasn't surprised when Talbern giggled at it.

I looked at her.

"It's okay. I'm used to people laughing. My parents should've changed it back in the sixties."

"Sorry," she said.

Kelvin said, "We're here to see the body."

"Sure. Which one of you is in charge here?"

Marksy stepped forward and said, "That'd be me."

Shpoik nodded and said, "Good to meet you. Listen, we don't have a real morgue, just a cold storage room. It's pretty small. We're not all going to fit."

Kelvin said, "I'll wait out here."

Marksy looked at Talbern and me. She said, "Talbern, stay out too. Widow, I guess it's going to be just you and me."

I shrugged.

We followed Shpoik out of the office and back down the hall to another door. We walked through what looked like a small critical care unit and past some nurses and one patient. Then he stopped and pulled open a heavy door with rubber around it, sealing it shut. The door sucked open, and we walked through.

Shpoik flicked on an overhead light from a switch on the wall and waited for us all to enter the room.

He closed the door behind us.

"That's her," he said without pointing, but she was obvious.

Karen Dekker lay on one of two metal tables in the center of the room.

Marksy asked, "You've positively IDed her, right?"

"Yes, it's Dekker. No doubt in my mind."

Silence fell over the room.

Shpoik said, "I just saw her a month ago."

"How's that?"

"It's a small base. She came to me for a checkup."

I asked, "Physical?"

"Of course."

"Why?"

"She was leaving. She got orders to go overseas. SOP is for every soldier to get a checkup before they fly."

I nodded.

"She was a good person."

Marksy asked, "How well did you know her?"

"Not socially. Just, you know, around the base. That sort of thing."

"How do you know she was a good person?"

The doctor shrugged and said, "She's dead. What do you want me to say about her? She was nice to me. Nice to my staff."

I tuned them out for a moment, stood over Dekker.

Her body was as bad as the other AWOL victims had been described in the case reports.

I heard Marksy ask, "You take out the bullet?"

"Nine millimeters. Like the others."

"Does it match any gun?"

"It doesn't match any specific weapon, but I'd say it was shot from a Beretta M9, just like the ones from two years ago."

I recalled reading that in the case report. The problem

was every Army service member had an issued M9. The one that was issued to Dayard didn't match. But that didn't clear him of anything. M9s could be purchased at just about any gun show or gun store in the country.

Marksy took an irritated breath inward and said, "Doctor, I'm asking you to tell me whether the bullet matches the bullets that killed the others? Was it the same gun?"

Shpoik nodded, said, "I apologize. I'm tired. Been working non-stop ever since she came in."

Marksy tilted her head, showing her impatience.

"I couldn't answer that. I can only tell you it's a nine millimeter. You'd have to send it to a lab for analysis."

"You haven't done that yet?"

"We don't have that here. Hamilton will have to send it off to Fort Keys to have them look at it."

Marksy said, "We can do it faster. Send it to our guys in Jacksonville."

"You can take it with you."

Marksy's temples turned an angry shade of red. She said, "You'd just hand it off to us? Just like that?"

"I meant that we'd have to ask Hamilton to clear it first. Of course."

"Just have him send it off to Jacksonville."

Shpoik nodded.

I studied Dekker for another ten minutes, paid little attention to the rest of their conversation.

I looked at her from top to bottom, looking for clues.

I closed my eyes, pulled up the slides of the dead women in my mind that I had seen back in New York. They clicked past from one to the next. I heard the *CHIK CHIK* sound as each horrifying image passed by like Pawn was in my brain clicking them on.

I visualized each dead body until they fit inside each other like faceless composites, all combined to make one dead woman.

I opened my eyes and stared at Dekker one last time. Every minute detail of her injuries and the bullet hole fit the MO of AWOL killer down to the details.

It was him—no doubt about it.

29

Marksy and the doctor finished their conversation. The doctor agreed to send off the bullet, to email photos of the body, and to keep Marksy in the loop on any new findings.

We left the base. Kelvin drove us down the highway and then onto the interstate. We headed south, how I came yesterday.

I could've made my way back to Cocoa Beach from here pretty easily. The thought occurred to me. But then it left because Talbern spoke.

"Where do we go now? Back to New York?"

Marksy said, "We should call Pawn. See where we stand."

"We should stop for coffee?" I said.

Everyone turned to look at me, except for Kelvin. He kept his eyes on the road.

"That's a good idea. Let's get off the interstate at the next town. See if we can find a McDonald's or something."

Kelvin nodded to her and drove another fifteen minutes. He got off the interstate and headed onto an exit that had no town name, only a street. But there were hotels and fast-food joints and gas stations everywhere.

We ended up sitting outside on the patio of a coffee chain called Roasted Bean.

I had a tall black coffee. Everyone else had what I had predicted they would have. Kelvin had a black coffee with a ton of sugar. Marksy had an espresso. And Talbern drank a strawberry smoothie.

Marksy stepped away and called Pawn.

We sat in silence for a while until Kelvin finally said, "I'm going to drive back to Jacksonville."

"What do you mean? Why?"

He shrugged, said, "There's no reason for us to be a part of this. Unless Pawn needs us."

Talbern said, "I'm not going back. Not yet."

Kelvin said nothing.

Marksy came back and sat down. She shot the rest of her espresso.

"What did he say?" Talbern asked.

"He thinks we should stay here for another day or so. See if anything new turns up. We'll have to get a couple of hotel rooms. Probably should head to Orlando."

Kelvin didn't mention his ideas of returning to his field office, but I could see it on his face. It made me wonder if he was jealous of Talbern and me. He did kind of act like a jealous boyfriend, like a third wheel.

Suddenly Talbern's phone rang, and she looked at the screen before answering it.

I guessed she didn't recognize the caller because she looked at me, confused.

She stood up and stepped away, answered the phone.

"FBI. Talbern here."

Silence.

"Who is this?"

Another pause as she listened.

"Oh."

She walked back and stared at me.

"It's for you."

I stared at her for a second. Then I stood up and took the phone, pressed it to my ear.

"Hello?"

"Widow? This is Clayton."

"What's up?"

"Dayard wants to see you. He has information."

"Why can't he just tell you?"

"Not Secretary Dayard. I'm talking about James. The son."

James is the one in prison.

"What's he got?"

"I got no idea. He won't say. He won't tell me or his father."

"Why me?" I asked, but I already suspected it was because he saw me as his last chance to get off death row.

Clayton said, "His father told him about you. I'm sure you know the rest."

"I'm pretty far away right now."

"Where are you?"

"We're in Florida."

"I see. What's the nearest airport? I'll buy you a ticket."

I took the phone away from my ear and covered the receiver. I looked at Talbern.

"It's Dayard. The one in prison. He wants us to go see him."

"We should do it. We're not doing anything here."

I nodded and spoke back into the phone.

"Clayton, don't bother. We'll head that way. The FBI will send me."

"I don't know if he'll talk in front of them."

"Tough shit. That's the way it is. It's their case."

"Okay. I would leave now if I were you. He made it sound urgent."

"Got it. Anything else?"

"No," he said, and hung up.

I gave the phone back to Talbern.

"We going?"

I walked with her back to the table and said, "We gotta go. Talbern and I have to go see Dayard."

Marksy looked up and said, "What the hell for?"

"He has evidence. He claims. Says he'll only show it to me."

Marksy said nothing.

Kelvin said, "You two better go. We can drive you to the airport in Orlando."

Marksy nodded, said, "I'm still not convinced that Dayard is innocent in all of this. He's got an accomplice. But maybe if we play along, he'll give up something useful, and we can solve this thing. So, go to him. Find out what he knows. I want to catch this guy before he does it again."

I nodded.

"Let's get going then," Kelvin said.

We all finished our drinks, except for Talbern. She took hers with us.

We threw away our trash in a trash can outside and hopped back into the SUV. We drove, listening to pop music most of the way to Orlando.

On our way, Marksy called her office back in New York and had them book Talbern and me on a commercial flight at four pm, which was about forty minutes after they dropped us off at the terminal.

We had no bags to check. We headed in and walked up to a machine. Talbern printed out boarding passes, and then we walked right to security. I got in line, and Talbern pulled me out of it.

She said, "We don't stand in line."

"I should fly with you more often."

She smiled, walked us to the priority pass line, where there was no one but a bored-looking TSA agent.

"Can I help you?" He asked.

Talbern pulled out her badge and said, "FBI."

She handed him the boarding passes.

He looked at her badge and inspected it. Then he asked, "Are you armed?"

"Yes."

"I need to print you a pass for your weapon."

"Fine."

"What about him? He FBI?"

"No. He's with me."

"Can I see his passport?"

I reached in my pocket and pulled it out, handed it over to him.

"Let me get my supervisor on the radio."

He called his supervisor, and we listened to the whole back and forth for a few minutes. Then we waited for another ten, and finally, the guy showed up and said, "Follow me."

We followed him through security, and he handed Talbern back her badge and gave my passport to me.

He gave Talbern a slip of paper.

"Carry this with you and show it to the pilot when you board. "We'll inform him you'll fly on his plane with your weapon, but you should show him this, anyway."

"Thanks," Talbern said, and she grabbed my hand, pulled me behind her.

We boarded the plane. Talbern followed the protocol. The pilot shook her hand and said nothing else about it.

I was disappointed in the flight because we were sitting in a coach. We went from a private jet and flight crew to sitting in coach.

It made me feel like a rich guy who lost it all at the track one night. It was quite the letdown.

I sat in a middle seat, and Talbern squeezed next to me at the window.

Suddenly, I realized I never asked what prison Dayard was in.

I asked, "Where the hell are we going?"

"Kansas."

"Kansas?" I asked.

"Yeah. That's where Dayard is."

"Wait. He's in Leavenworth?"

"Yeah. He was an Army officer who murdered three soldiers. Where else would he go?"

"Pawn said he was on death row. Said he was getting executed."

"What about it?"

"The military hasn't executed an inmate on death row since nineteen sixty-one."

We had a three-hour flight and landed at Kansas City International Airport and rented a car. Talbern put everything on a credit card that I assumed belonged to the FBI.

We drove out to Fort Leavenworth.

The thing that Leavenworth is most famous for is the prison, naturally. But I was pretty stunned by how beautiful the town of Leavenworth, Kansas, and the fort was.

There were rolling hills, lush greenery everywhere, and huge blue skies.

The town was built overlooking the Missouri River. There were gothic American-style buildings and streets. London-style street lamps from the nineteenth century burned everywhere as the night came on. They were all-electric and not torchlight, like the old London ones, of course.

I watched out the window as we drove through the town and up to the fort. That was as much sightseeing as I was going to get. I was sure.

We came up to the gate.

Fort Leavenworth was an entire world from the tiny base of Graham. It was heavily guarded compared to Graham.

Even with Talbern's badge, we had to go through a whole rigmarole before we were even allowed on base. And that's counting the fact that Pawn had called ahead and told the MPs to expect us.

Eventually, we had to get out of the vehicle. We couldn't drive it onto the base. We had to leave it at a check-in center in front of the west gate.

They assigned a liaison to us. A Warrant Officer named Pines. She was a female officer in her early thirties. She was Hispanic and short, around five-three. She was shorter than Talbern, but not much.

She had tightly cropped hair, black, and a great smile. She was warm and friendly.

She picked us up at the gate in a military police car, a Ford Crown Vic.

Talbern sat next to her in the front, which left the rear bench for me. I smiled before getting in. Talbern looked at me and smiled back. She knew why it was funny. She didn't have to ask.

Pines looked back at me over her shoulder.

She said, "It's nice to meet both of you."

"Likewise," I said.

Talbern kept her smile on her face and targeted it at Pines instead of at me.

"You guys are interviewing the AWOL killer like before he's gone or something?"

"What do you know about him, Pines?" I asked.

"Just like everyone else. You know, I followed it on the news."

Talbern asked, "What's he like?"

"Oh, I never met him. This will be my first time. I've heard he's disappointing."

"Disappointing?" Talbern asked,

"Yeah, like he's normal. Quiet, even."

"The quiet man."

"What?" she asked.

"Nothing. Never mind. Does he ever claim he's innocent?"

"All the time. They all do."

Talbern said, "Has he made any friends inside?"

"Friends?"

"Does he talk to anyone? Interact with other prisoners?"

"He can't. He's kept in solitary."

"Why?" I asked.

"Not really solitary. It's just that he has his own cell. He's kept on the block with the other death row inmates."

"I thought the Army had executed no one for like fifty years. But they have a block for soldiers on death row?" Talbern asked.

Pines cringed. I could see it on her face. She didn't like that Talbern had called Dayard a soldier and not a prisoner. To folks in the military, you commit a crime; then you disgraced the uniform. Thus disqualifying you to be called a soldier. But Pines said nothing about it.

"Since nineteen sixty It's true. But because of the nature of Dayard's crimes, no judge will grant a stay of execution."

"Nineteen sixty-one was the year."

They both looked at me, Pines from the rearview and Talbern over her shoulder.

She said, "Don't mind him."

Pines didn't respond. She moved her eyes forward and drove on.

I stared out the window as we turned and drove down several streets. It seemed like she was taking us the back way to the prison.

It turned out she was. Instead of going in through the main entrance, through the numerous guards posted and gate checks, we came in through a separate gate. It was for deliveries. There still were MPs in armored vests and helmets and carrying serious AR15 rifles.

They saluted Pines and let us through with little delay.

Pines drove the car into a big lot and parked it near a covered Army truck in the back.

We got out and followed her through a series of security doors with sliding card entry. Finally, we ended up taking an elevator up to the third floor. We got off and walked down a long, Army green hallway.

There was a red stripe painted down the corridor.

She stopped in front of a heavy metal door and turned back to us.

"This is it."

I reached out and grabbed her arm gently.

"Mind if we see him alone?"

Talbern looked up at me but didn't protest.

"Well. Um," Pines said. She looked down at her watch, like the answer was on the face of it.

"It's important to the bureau that we can interview the subject with no military presence."

"Why?"

Talbern added, "We were told that we could interview

him alone. It's a matter of life or death. He has information that can help a separate case."

Pines looked at Talbern for a sign of honesty in what she was saying. Pines wasn't stupid.

I let go of her arm, and Talbern kept a straight face.

"Okay," Pines agreed.

She turned the doorknob and led us into the room.

There was an MP standing guard at another door, inside the room, on the opposite wall. She walked over to him. He saluted her, and she spoke to him out of earshot.

He turned and nodded an affirmative response to her, then he opened the other door and exited.

She walked back to us and said, "He'll be here in a moment. I told them to give you privacy. But remember, the cameras stay on."

She looked up at a camera in one corner of the room.

"We never turn those off."

Talbern and I both stared up at the camera. It was a big, ugly gray thing with a huge lens on the end. It looked like it was the original model, installed over fifty years ago.

"We don't even turn those off for lawyer meetings," Pines said.

Talbern said, "Really?"

"Soldiers don't get lawyer-client privileges," I said. "At least not the way you think of it."

Talbern shrugged.

I said, "In boot camp, the drill instructors say your asses belong to the Army. That's exactly what they mean."

Pines reached her hand out and shook Talbern's. She said, "Okay. Just knock on the door when you're ready. I'll be outside."

And she turned and left us.

In the center of the room was a metal table. It reminded

me of the table that Dekker's body was displayed on back in Florida. Only this one wasn't so polished. It was faded like it had intentionally been painted matte metallic gray.

There were three chairs at the table. One on the prisoner's side, I figured, and two for visitors.

Talbern took a seat without me. I stayed standing. I was a tall guy, and I found most people were intimidated by my size when they first meet me. I wanted Dayard to see my size. I didn't want him to see me sitting and lose a major advantage that I have over most people.

We waited for about five minutes, and then we saw the door on the inside of the room dribble open in an overly slow pace.

James Dayard walked in. He stood a whole hell of a lot shorter than I had imagined. He was about five-four, a whole foot shorter than me, and within an inch of Talbern.

He had a tall crop of hair, platinum blond. The sides were shaved to his skin, but the top was one of those old fedora style cuts, where it waves up and over, like a comic book superhero.

His hair had tremendous depth. He looked like he had just walked out of a salon instead of a high-security prison.

He wore black, square glasses with ultra-thin lenses.

Dayard was a serious smoker, or he was hanging out with one because I could smell fresh cigarette smoke on his clothes from across the room.

He wore the traditional orange jumpsuit.

I saw a guard behind him shove him through the door and retreat into the hall, shut the door.

Dayard wasn't shackled or restrained.

He entered and nodded at us.

He said, "I hear that you're here to save me?"

30

DAYARD SAT down across from Talbern and smiled crookedly at her. One of his front teeth was chipped, but he seemed nice enough.

"How did you hear that?" I asked.

"I'm sure you know."

I walked over and pulled the chair out next to Talbern, dumped myself down in it.

"We need to know the truth," Talbern said. She didn't seem nervous, but I sensed she might've been. I imagined it wasn't every day a sophomore FBI agent gets this close to a convicted serial killer.

"The truth?" he asked. I sensed some emotion in his response. Not anger, not flat out anyway, but it was more like sadness.

I stayed quiet.

"Do you know who has picked up your mantle?"

Dayard's face went flush. He looked at the back of his hands. They were white and clean, like a man who had never worked before in his life, which amazed me. He had been in the Army, made it through officer school, and worked his way up to the rank of major. I didn't see how it was possible for him to have such unmarked hands.

"No one has picked up my mantle. He's just continuing his own work."

"Do you still claim that you're innocent?"

He slammed his hands down on the table.

"I am innocent!"

I paused a beat, stared into his eyes. He was convincing.

"Calm down," I commanded in my old cop voice.

He stayed quiet.

"We need your help. Who is this guy? Who's killing now?"

"I got no idea."

"Tell us the truth," Talbern said.

"I am telling you the truth."

Talbern waited for a moment, and then she said, "James, if you help us, we can help you?"

"Help me what?"

"We can talk to the Army. Get you off death row."

He laughed.

"Lady, I could get me off death row now."

"How's that?"

"I got enough proof to produce doubt. I could tell a judge that you came to see me. I can tell them that there's been a new murder victim. How could I kill anyone if I'm locked up in here?"

He knows there's a victim, which didn't really surprise me. I'm sure Clayton or his father has been getting updates from someone.

A look of checkmate came over his face, like he still had an ace up his sleeve.

Talbern caught onto it. I could see it.

She asked, "What's that look for?"

"I want you to believe me. That I'm innocent. I never killed anyone."

Silence.

"I have proof."

"What proof?"

"I have actual proof," he said.

I asked, "What is it?"

Dayard leaned forward and stood up.

Talbern reached into her coat, fast, unsnapped the safety button on her holster, and grabbed the hilt of her Glock. She was ready to brandish it and shoot Dayard dead. All a quick precaution in case he tried to attack us with a concealed weapon. But he didn't pull a weapon out.

Instead, he slowed his movement and reached into the inside of his shirt, pulled out a thin stack of cards. They looked like postcards.

He tossed them onto the table in front of us.

Talbern relaxed her hand and asked, "What're these?"

"Take a look."

Talbern picked up the stack of cards and looked them over.

I kept my eyes on Dayard, in case this was a trick. Easily, he could show us a bunch of nonsense cards, and leap at us, going for Talbern's Glock. Now he knew where it was, and he had seen her unsnap the safety button on it.

Talbern kept her eyes locked on the cards.

I took a quick glance down to confirm what they were. Then I looked back at Dayard.

They were postcards.

"Widow, look at this."

Talbern shoved the postcards at me.

I took them and looked them over.

There were maybe a dozen.

I stared down at them. Each was stamped from different parts of Mexico and South America. All except for the most recent one. It was postmarked out of Miami.

Each one had a short handwritten phrase. The first was, "How's prison?"

The second was, "How's the food?"

The third was, "Made any friends?"

I breezed through the next several. They were all short taunts, like the first three. I scanned them until I got to the most recent one.

It was dated with yesterday's date like it had come in the mail just now.

It read: I couldn't help myself.

31

"They're from the real killer," Dayard said.

I looked them over again, more closely this time. Kept my fingers along the edges, in case there was forensic evidence. The earliest one was dated a year ago.

"That's your real killer."

"How long have you gotten these?" Talbern asked.

"A year," I said. "That's the oldest one."

"Why didn't you tell anyone?"

Dayard slammed his palms down on the table again.

"I did! I showed my lawyer! I showed the warden! They don't believe me!"

"Why didn't you demand that your lawyer give this to the FBI?" Talbern asked.

"He says he did!"

I stared at Dayard, tried to read him. I was getting the same impression. He was convincing.

I asked, "Did they look at them for fingerprints?"

He shook his head; then he turned his attention to Talbern. He pointed his finger at her. "It's that Agent Marksy! She dismissed them!"

He paused a beat, and then he said, "She's the reason that I'm in here! She framed me!"

Silence.

Talbern asked, "You don't believe that?"

"It's true! The witness that supposedly saw me with his wife! That was bullshit! He never even knew about us until she told him!"

"How did you get these back?" I asked.

"Marksy sent them all back in a folder. No message. No word about any fingerprints. Nothing."

I nodded.

We were quiet for a long moment.

Talbern said, "Mr. Dayard, thanks for cooperating. We need to discuss all this."

"Thank you," he responded.

We stood up first. Dayard stayed seated.

Talbern asked, "Mind if we take these?"

"Take them."

We started to walk out, but Dayard cleared his throat and said, "Agent lady."

We turned back to him.

"Work fast. I ain't got but two days left."

Talbern nodded, and we knocked on the door.

Pines opened it and led us out of the room and down the long hall, back out of the prison.

32

WE DIDN'T TALK about the postcards until we were back out of the gate. Pines seemed disappointed. She kept asking us questions, but we didn't answer them. I said nothing the whole ride back out. And Talbern just answered with pleasantries.

Outside the gate and back in the rented car, Talbern said, "Widow, no one at the FBI knows about these postcards."

"That's not surprising. If Dayard handed them to his lawyer and they actually gave them to the FBI, it would've been to the agent in charge of the investigation. That'd be Marksy. She wanted him dead for killing her husband. She would've sent them straight back to him. She probably never even scanned them or logged them in."

"What do we do?"

"I doubt she knows about the latest one. And I can't blame her for ignoring them before."

"And now?"

"It's compelling."

Talbern nodded, said, "We've gotta call Pawn."

"I think you should call Marksy first. Tell her about the new one."

"You think she'll take them seriously this time?"

"This time is different. We got a dead body now."

Talbern nodded.

We drove through the cozy town of Leavenworth for a long time until we stopped at a red light. Talbern asked, "Where to now? The airport?"

"Let's make the phone calls first. Then we'll know where to go."

"Let me guess; you want coffee?"

"Coffee is always a good idea."

She nodded, and we drove around looking for a diner, but Talbern saw a Starbucks.

We went in and stood in line for what seemed like forever. The store was, like many of the ones I had seen before, over-crowded and far too small.

It was a nice day outside, so we ended up taking a coffee and a bottle of juice, and we sat on the hood of the car in the parking lot. We faced the highway.

There was an overpass that whirred every few seconds from cars passing over it.

"Do you believe his story?" she asked.

"Do you?"

"I'm asking you."

I shrugged.

"I wasn't totally convinced."

"About which part? The postcards?"

"I don't know. That seems very menacing and sinister. Like it's out of a Lee Grisham novel."

"Who?"

"Isn't that the name of the writer who does those thrillers?"

"I don't know?"

"He's from your state?"

"John Grisham."

"Right. Sorry."

I shrugged.

She drank half of her bottle of green juice. I wasn't sure what the hell it was.

Then she got up and pulled out her cellphone. It was ringing on vibrate. She must've turned it on vibrate back in the prison.

"It's Marksy," she said, and she answered it and stepped a couple of paces toward the highway.

"We're still here," she said.

Then Marksy must've spoken, because she listened.

"He told us about the postcards."

Silence.

"I don't know. There's a new one. I think we need to take it seriously."

She was quiet again.

"Listen, the new one is from Miami."

Talbern said nothing else, just nodded along like Marksy was here looking at her.

She clicked off the phone.

"That was fast," I said.

"She brought up the postcards, right off."

"And?"

"And you're right. She knew about them and dismissed them. She really has it in for Dayard."

"What did she say now?"

"She agrees we should take them seriously."

I asked, "So what's the next move?"

"She said to hang tight. She's going to call Pawn. See what he wants us to do."

I nodded, finished my coffee, and crumbled up the cup. I slid off the hood of the car and started walking away, looking for a wastebasket.

"There's one over there," Talbern said and pointed at a pillar.

The trashcan was behind it. I tossed the coffee cup in and walked back to her.

"Want to check out the town?"

"I think we should go to the airport. We'll need to fly out soon. I'm sure."

I shrugged.

We got in the car and headed back to the airport.

33

SITTING NEXT to each other on airport chairs, fused together by metal rails, we waited for Talbern's phone to ring.

It was taking a while for Marksy to call us back. Like most airports across the country that I had ever been to, Kansas City International Airport was freezing. Talbern noticed I was cold.

"You should buy some new clothes here."

"I don't know. Airport shops are overpriced beyond overpriced," I said.

She smiled and pulled out a billfold. It was a tiny black thing that matched her shoes. She said, "Here. Let us pay for it."

I stood up and turned back to her, took the end of a credit card that she had stretched out to me.

"Are you sure?"

She shrugged.

"Of course. It's the least we can do."

"Thanks. I'll just try around the corner."

"Take your time. I'll come to find you."

I walked away and turned a corner. I passed people on

cellphones, pulling carry-on travel bags, and trafficking along in hurried manners.

American airports are what shopping malls used to be twenty years ago. They were palaces of department stores, filled with varying groups of people who ignored each other.

I passed a Hudson News store and a doughnut shop, and finally, I found a store that had some clothing in it.

It was all top name brands.

I passed a man dressed in a suit. He must've been the store clerk because he looked me up and then down. He had a look of judgment on his face, which I couldn't blame him for. I was walking around, sporting sneakers and surfer pants.

I looked around. Like most men, the first thing I looked at was the price tags. Everything was expensive. Glad I wasn't paying for any of it.

Then I smiled because the thought of government funding came to mind.

Might as well splurge a little. Then I thought I might need something tactical.

I looked through the pants first. They were all nice trousers. To me, dress slacks are dress slacks. The only difference really is the fit.

I had another thought. I thought about Clayton. I thought about all those guys dressed like Secret Service agents.

Why the hell did Dayard need so many agents?

I know I asked Clayton that question, back in the helicopter, or the car. I couldn't remember which. He had said that Secretary Dayard had a long career. He had made a lot of enemies.

I accepted that answer. But then I remembered seeing floodlights and cameras and some other security measures in the house.

Why all that?

I looked back across the store for a section with jeans. They didn't have any. I settled for a pair of black chinos. Pulled them off the rack and checked the size and the fit. It looked good.

Then I walked over to undershirts. All they offered were black and white t-shirts. Each pair was singled out and folded. They weren't in a package deal like I was used to.

I found an extra-large black one and scooped it up. Next to that, I found black socks and single pairs of underwear, briefs.

I looked at the dress shirts and tried to find something in all black.

As I sifted through their inventory, my mind raced back to that house.

What was Dayard afraid of?

The question nagged at me like a splinter.

For a moment, I thought, what if James Dayard was telling the truth? What if he had been framed for the murders? By whom?

"Would you like for me to start a fitting room for you, sir?"

I craned my head and looked back over my shoulder.

The store clerk was standing about a meter behind me. Now he had a smile on his face. The reason for the smile was that he wasn't alone.

Talbern stood behind him.

The clerk said, "Your wife said that you'd like to try those on first."

My wife? I thought.

"Yes. I need a fitting room, please. Thanks for the suggestion, honey," I said to Talbern.

"You're welcome, dear. But, hey, we should hurry."

"Something up?"

"I got a text from Kelvin. He said that Marksy was going to call soon."

I nodded.

She looked at the shirt I was holding and stepped close to me. She snatched it out of my hand and said, "Not that one."

She put it back on the rack and picked up a short-sleeved black knit shirt instead. She handed it to me.

"Try this one."

"Thanks."

I gave it all to the store clerk, who took it and vanished into a small, thin door in the back corner of the store. The fitting room, I figured.

He came back out and asked, "Do you need shoes?"

"Where are they?"

"Over there on the mannequin. We only have one style. What size would you like?"

I looked at the display mannequin he was talking about. There was a pair of black, shiny loafers on its fake plastic feet.

I told him my size, and his eyes opened wide.

"Not sure if we have that size. I'll take a look. You can go into the fitting room. I'll bring them back to you."

I nodded and went back into the fitting room. It was the smallest fitting room that I had ever seen. There was no area for employees to fold or work. It was just a single stall with a lockless door on it.

I went in and put on the clothes. Everything was a perfect fit. I especially liked the pants. They were comfortable and had good quality.

The clerk returned with the shoes and passed them to me. He added a pair of socks.

Both fit well.

I walked out of the fitting room.

Talbern stared at me up and down.

"You look like a different man, Jack Widow."

"Thanks," I said.

I looked at the clerk and said, "I'll take all of it."

I gave him the card and paid for everything. Talbern signed. She didn't even bat an eye at the price. I almost had a heart attack when I saw the number. I never bought a single set of clothing for three digits in an airport before.

I tore off all the tags that I could find. Talbern saw I intended to wear it all out, so she pulled off a couple of stickers that I didn't see.

"What about your clothes, sir?" the clerk asked.

"Keep 'em," I said and turned and walked out with Talbern next to me.

34

We randomly waited by Gate D1, which was harboring passengers waiting on a flight to Jamaica. I would be lying if I said that I wasn't tempted to forget this whole thing and get on that flight instead. The thought occurred to me to convince Talbern to come with me. We could spend our days lying on the beach, rolling in the sand, and catching the waves.

I imagined Talbern in a bikini. I imagined her tanned to a bronze finish like a Greek Goddess.

I smiled to myself, but Talbern caught me.

"What're you smiling about?"

"I was just thinking about you."

"Thinking about me?"

"And Jamaica and bikinis."

She asked, "Why do you think about that?"

I pointed at the flight information posted on a digital monitor.

"Jamaica sounds good," she said.

She paused, lowered her head into my shoulder, and whispered, "I never smoked weed. Not once."

"That's not a bad thing," I said.

"Have you ever?"

Instead of a flat out answer, I said, "Maybe."

She smiled. She looked like she was going to say something else, but her phone rang in her pocket.

She sat up straight and pulled it out, answered it.

"Talbern."

She listened.

"Yeah. We're at the airport now."

She listened some more.

"Okay, where does he want us to go?"

I got Talbern's attention and mouthed, "Let me talk."

She nodded and continued to listen for a long moment.

"Marksy, Widow wants to talk."

She handed me the phone.

"What's up, Widow?" Marksy said.

"Talbern told you about the postcards?"

"She did."

"I know you disregarded them before, but there's a new one. From Miami."

Silence.

I said, "What if they're for real?"

She stayed quiet.

"Someone is really sending them."

"Right. What do you suggest I do?"

"First off, someone needs to confiscate them from Dayard. Send them to the lab. I know it's a longshot, but you never know."

"I agree. What did you think of Dayard?"

"Not sure. But something has been bothering me."

Marksy asked, "What's that?"

Silence fell between us. I thought for a long second about Dayard and the extra protection, again.

"Widow?"

"Listen, we need to talk in person."

"I'm already sending you guys back down here to Orlando."

I said, "No. Not Florida."

Marksy paused, and then she said, "Pawn wants us to stay down here. There's still a lot of work to be done, with Dekker. There're clues still here."

"Kelvin can handle Dekker. I need to see you in person, and we need to go to Portland."

"Why the hell do you want to go there?"

"I'll tell you in person."

"Widow, when I tell Pawn about the postcards, he's going to order us to stay down here. He'll say what it looks like."

I said nothing.

She said, "You know that there's a real killer out there who has been living his life free in the Caribbean, while Dayard rots on death row. I'm telling you he won't let us go anywhere else."

"Just do it. Meet us in Portland."

Silence fell over the line again. I heard Marksy breathing. She was thinking.

"It's almost six here. I won't even meet you guys until midnight."

"Just get there. Call Talbern when you land."

"See you there," she said and hung up the line.

I gave the phone back to Talbern. She looked at the screen and exited the phone app.

"What the hell is that about?"

"First, let's get tickets to Portland. We need to get there now," I said. "What time is it?"

After I asked the time, I forgot Marksy had just told me. Six on the east coast meant it was five here. Which Talbern told me.

"Get the fastest tickets. Nonstop. Okay?"

"Okay, want to tell me what's going on?"

"After. Get the tickets first."

She nodded, and we walked back out of the gate area, back to the ticket counters. She purchased two tickets to Portland. The only nonstop didn't leave for another two hours. The flight length was four and a half hours, putting us on the ground in Portland just before midnight.

After we paid for the tickets, printed the boarding passes, and went back through security, repeating the whole official process of checking Talbern's Glock in with the TSA and getting the paperwork in order, we sat at a different gate this time.

We were flying with Delta, not first class, which I had been secretly hoping for, but premium economy, which wasn't that bad.

Instead of waiting for those airport seats, we found a Japanese restaurant and sat at a table.

Talbern had water and sushi.

I looked over the menu, found nothing that appealing, but they had coffee.

By the time she asked me to explain why we were going to Portland, I was starting on my second cup.

"What's going on? Why back to Portland?"

"I was thinking about Secretary Dayard."

"What about him?"

"When we were at the house, what did you see?"

She used a pair of chopsticks with no problems, like a professional. I saw the appeal of chopsticks. I used either my fingers or a fork. I didn't have an opinion on sushi. I didn't hate it like many people. I just thought little it.

"It was pretty lonely."

"What else?"

"It was bleak?"

"And?"

"I don't know. What else is there?"

"What about Dayard himself?"

"He was very sad."

"What else?"

Talbern took another bite and waited until she swallowed it to speak.

She said, "I don't know. What else is there?"

"Why did he have all that security?"

"He's a former politician?"

I said, "Not really. Secretary of Defense is an appointed position."

"There's still campaigning involved. Most choices have to campaign for the job."

"True, but why would he need all those guards? And they're former Secret Service, which means they are the best of the best."

Talbern shrugged, and said, "I don't know?"

"Fear," I said.

"Fear of what?"

"I stayed quiet."

She said, "He's afraid of something."

"He's afraid of someone," I said.

"Who?"

"What else did you see in the house?"

She looked down at the table and then back at me.

"He lost his family."

"His whole family," I said.

"His wife died giving birth. His oldest son killed himself."

I took another pull from my coffee and asked, "How did he do it?"

"He," she said, but then she stopped. She started thinking.

"I don't know how. He drowned himself. I guess."

I took a last pull of the coffee, drain it.

I repeated, "Did he?"

She looked at me.

"Are you saying he's not dead?"

"They never found a body."

"You think John, Jr. is alive? He's the AWOL killer?"

I stayed quiet.

"Is that possible?"

"Anything is possible."

"Why are we going to Portland? Are we going to ask Secretary Dayard to his face?"

I said, "One thing at a time. First, we need to see the weather reports from the times of deaths of the other three victims. Precisely. I need to see when their bodies were found?"

"What for?"

"Can you get that for me?"

"Sure. I'll call Marksy back."

"No. Call Pawn directly. I don't want her getting distracted from meeting us. I need to speak to her in person."

"What do I tell him it's for?"

"Just the truth."

"Do I tell him that John, Jr. might be alive?"

I nodded.

"Don't tell anyone that part. We know nothing. Just tell him I've gotta hunch. Okay?"

"Okay. What else do we need?" she asked and paused.

I was about to speak, but she interrupted.

She said, "There was a transmission from John before he killed himself. The Coast Guard recorded it. We should get a copy of that."

"It can't hurt. But I will need something. When we land."

"What's that?"

"A gun."

35

Hours later, Talbern was fast asleep, next to me on the plane to Portland. She had offered me the window seat this time. She insisted on it. I didn't fight her.

I stared out of the window. We were nearing Portland, about a half-hour out, I figured.

The sky was dark and pouring rain. Lightning crashed in the distance, below the clouds.

Talbern hadn't said a word about getting me a gun, but I thought of how to get one without her if I had to.

We were going up against an unknown enemy. *The John Jr. Theory* seemed farfetched, but Dayard had said that he had flunked out of the Army because of psychological reasons. If he had faked his own death and was killing women, all while blaming it on his younger brother, then John Jr. was a little crazy.

That made him very dangerous. A psychotic killer was one of the worst kinds of suspects to catch. They're unpredictable. And so far, John Jr. had the upper hand on everyone else.

If he was alive and was guilty of the AWOL murders,

then he had fooled everyone for a long time. He fooled his dad, his brother, the Army, and the FBI. He wasn't to be underestimated.

I needed a gun.

Talbern had fallen asleep and was laying her head on my shoulder, which felt nice.

I didn't wake her. But the pilot had come over the intercom and announced that we were descending.

She woke up. Her eyes were groggy.

"Did I fall asleep on you?"

"For a bit."

"So sorry."

"I liked it," I said.

She said nothing to that.

She had uncrossed her arms and sat up straight. She raised her seat to the upright position, and we both looked out the window as we came in for a landing.

The wind and rain pounded outside as the landing gear came down and rolled to a stop on the runway.

36

WE WAITED at Gate C10 in Portland Airport for Marksy's plane to arrive.

She was scheduled to land just ten minutes after us.

While we waited, Talbern called Pawn. She explained to him what was going on, but she left out the possibility that John Jr. might be alive. She just made it seem like I had a hunch and wouldn't give it all away just yet.

He sent the reports on the weather that I asked for.

Talbern came over to me, said, "Take the phone. I downloaded the weather reports for the days of the murders. You can read over it over there. I'll wait for Marksy."

"Okay," I said. I took the phone and found an empty chair near a huge window.

The rain poured down, echoing a steady static sound that raindrops made on glass.

I looked through the weather reports in Talbern's email.

There was three-days' worth of reports around each murder and when the bodies were found. The total was twelve days of weather.

I saw right away the pattern that I was expecting.

I got up and walked back over to Talbern.

"Her flights late," Talbern said, looking down at her watch.

"How long?"

"Twenty minutes."

"She'll be here. Check this out," I said. I handed her the phone with the weather reports open.

She sifted through it and asked, "What am I looking for?"

"What do you see?"

She looked at the first two murders and then the third.

"Every time AWOL killed someone, it was during a thunderstorm."

"Yep."

"What does that mean?"

"He kills in cycles. Weather cycles."

"Okay, but what does that prove?"

"Dekker," I said.

"What about her?"

"This is just one more thing that the killer did exactly the same."

She asked, "Did it rain when Dekker was murdered?"

"Yes. I know. I was only miles from where she was found. It had been raining at sea for a couple of days. It rolled up on the beach while I was there. I saw it."

"So this just adds another layer to it. Does this prove that John, Jr. is our guy?"

I shrugged and said, "No. It just proves that whoever killed Dekker has intimate knowledge of the exact circumstances of whoever really killed those others."

"Marksy is going to look like she fumbled everything at the end of this."

I stayed quiet.

"Is that why you want her here?"

"I just want to ask her something."

Talbern didn't press me about what.

We waited, and a few minutes later, people piled out of the gate.

Marksy was near the front. She walked over to us. She looked tired but didn't complain about it.

"I'm here. Let's get going to wherever we are supposed to be going, Widow."

I nodded, and we left the airport.

We waited for a taxi. We found one and got in. Marksy sat next to Talbern in the back, and I sat in the front with the driver.

"Where to?" He asked.

"The old Portland Harbor?"

"Which side?"

"The private docks," I said.

"You got it," the driver said, and he drove away from the curb.

"Why are we going to the docks?" Marksy asked.

Talbern spent a good part of the ride explaining to Marksy about Secretary Dayard. She told her about the dead son, the postcards, the weather, and about how it seems possible that John Jr. might not be dead.

Marksy listened. For a moment, she stared out the window, making me a little nervous because I thought maybe she wouldn't buy it.

"So why are we headed to the harbor?"

"We're going to see the family boat," I said.

"What?! Why?"

She was upset. Which was understandable because the boat was where her husband had been shot.

"The boat was where you thought you caught Dayard. It's where you confronted him, right?"

"Yes."

"And then he got away?"

"Yes. You already know this."

"When's the last time the FBI set foot on it?"

"I got no idea. I'm sure it's been for two years."

"So, it's not under protection?"

"No. Why would it be? The trial's been over. Dayard was convicted."

I asked, "What did you guys do with it after?"

"We returned it to Dayard. The father."

I nodded, said, "We met him."

"I already know that."

"Did you know he's dying?"

She was quiet.

"Secretary Dayard is at the end of his life. He's got cancer. Said it was terminal."

"Sorry to hear that. What's that got to do with his boat?"

"We saw him. We saw him up close."

"So?"

"He's not faking cancer. I've seen sick people before. He's really got it."

"So?" Marksy repeated.

"So, he's not using the boat."

"And?"

"And I doubt that he's even been to it since the FBI returned it."

"Okay?"

"Somebody might be."

Marksy said, "You think that John, Jr. is there?"

I shook my head, said, "No, I think that if he really is still alive, then he's in Florida somewhere or back in the Caribbean or at sea. He's probably been living on a boat.

"Dayard told us he killed himself out on a boat. Said that

he was a good sailor. So if he faked it, he might hide out on a boat somewhere. What better way to avoid detection than just going from country to country?"

Marksy said nothing.

Talbern asked, "What's the question that you wanted to ask?"

"Wait till we are there."

Talbern nodded, and Marksy looked at me with an expression that I could best describe as estrangement.

She wasn't the kind of FBI agent to wait for things. I gathered.

About forty minutes later, and we were driving into what looked like an abandoned port.

I looked out the window and realized that it stopped raining. It was still bleak and dreary out. Off in the distance, I saw a crackle of lightning. It reminded me of that day on Cocoa Beach.

We had passed the normal Portland Harbor and the business end of shipyards until we had driven through an old, forgotten neighborhood. Most of the houses looked either abandoned or damn close to it.

The driver pulled in and stopped at the gate.

"This is it," he said.

Marksy leaned forward and handed the guy two twenty-dollar bills. At first, he seemed happy about it, but then he saw she was waiting for her change.

He gave change, and she tipped him less than ten percent, by my calculation. That seemed to make him unhappy because he grunted at it.

I stepped out first and looked over the parking lot for the old boat harbor.

There were a couple of beat-up pickup trucks, three different old model Jeep Wranglers, and a black Ford sedan that stuck out because it was fairly new, compared to the rest of the vehicles in the lot.

The rest of the parking lot was abandoned.

"Where to?" I asked.

"I don't know," Talbern said. "I'll look it up. Gotta be in our records somewhere."

Marksy walked ahead, said, "No. Need. I've been here. Remember?"

Talbern nodded, slumped her shoulders. I could see that she felt bad about forgetting. It was on the Dayard boat that Marksy's husband was shot and killed.

The old Portland Harbor was quite large. It had several grids of piers that went out and mazed back, interconnecting.

I tried to lighten the mood and said, "Could be worse."

Marksy looked back over her shoulder at me.

"Could be raining still," I said.

She didn't respond, just looked forward and scanned the boats. She said, "This way. It's at the end."

We followed behind her.

I walked close to Talbern and said, "We never got me a gun."

"Think you'll need it here?"

"Probably, not. Better safe than sorry."

"I have a gun, and Marksy is armed. I'm sure we can cover you against a phantom."

I smiled.

I walked close to Talbern the whole way. We followed Marksy in a straight line until the shoreline of the harbor circled. Then we curved with it, passing boats as we walked.

The sea was rough and choppy, even this close in. Dozens and dozens of boats of all sizes swayed and rocked on the water.

City lights bounced off the water. I heard a far-off bell ringing from a buoy in the distance.

There was the faint sound of music and lights coming from the boat in the middle. Someone was home, watching TV on it.

The last section of boat slips was also the richest section. That was obvious, because the boats in this part were far bigger than the earlier ones.

There were old, but well-kept sailboats and yachts: nothing giant, but all pretty big.

We walked down the walkway toward the end.

Marksy stopped about three boats from the end. She shot her hand up, signaling us to stop. She drew her weapon, looked back at Talbern.

Marksy had the same model Glock that Talbern carried.

Talbern drew hers and put her hand out to me.

"Stay back," she whispered.

I nodded, with no intention of doing that.

Marksy lowered her stance. She approached the Dayard boat.

I had never seen the boat before, but I knew it was the last one because Marksy was locked onto it. Her eyes stared dead-on at the boat's bow.

I couldn't tell if there were lights on it or not, but I guessed that something made her draw her Glock.

Talbern and I stayed close behind and approached the sailboat, low.

As we got up on it, Marksy seemed to relax a bit. She stepped across the water and onto the deck. We followed.

"Keep back, Widow," she barked at me.

I crouched low to the deck and stayed where I was.

Marksy and Talbern checked out the rest of the deck, and then Marksy disappeared down below deck. They both clicked on flashlights. I saw the thin, bright beams pierce through a small window on the deck.

I stayed where I was.

Lightning crashed again. This time it spider-webbed across the underbelly of a huge system of storm clouds.

Then I heard something. Something faint. I turned back, stared down the pier. I heard a creak.

There was nothing there. The low *DING* of the bell from the buoy sounded over and over, slow and rhythmic.

The waves chopped and rushed below us.

I looked back at the flashlights below deck. Marksy and Talbern were still clearing the boat, making sure that it was safe and empty.

I should've insisted on a gun, I thought.

What if John Jr. was alive?

What if he was here? Waiting?

The animal brain part of me thought back to the parking lot.

The parking lot.

I thought about it for a moment and then dismissed it. But again, my instincts nagged at me.

That black Ford. It was new. It didn't belong.

I closed my eyes and tried to picture it. I looked inside through the front window. Two bumps from the front chairs, a rearview mirror, and nothing else. Right?

I checked the car before we came down here to the boat.

Didn't I?

Wait! I barely checked it out!

I remembered looking as we passed through the parking lot, but I didn't look close enough. I closed my eyes tighter and tried to recall the car.

I opened my eyes wide.

Someone was in it. I remembered it now. I had seen the

backs of the front chairs, but there were three, not two. Like someone had been slumping down in the middle.

I turned to look at the entrance leading below deck. I had to get Marksy and Talbern.

Then I heard the creak again from the pier. It came from behind me, but it was much, much closer.

I spun around and saw a man standing there on the pier. He was right behind me.

He wore all black. Black trousers. Black shirt. It was a good shirt, like mine. It was short-sleeved, like mine. But he wore a clip-on black tie. And he wore black leather driving gloves.

The guy had a SIG Sauer P229R tucked into the waistband of his trousers. And he was holding a Remington 870, which is a serious shotgun, trusted by the US Secret Service, among other international outfits.

The guy was tall. Shorter than me, but not much. He was lean, and I could see that he had serious, hard muscles from his exposed arms.

I knew he was armed with two serious guns, and I never got one. But the thing about the guy that raised the hairs on the back of my neck was that I couldn't see his face.

I couldn't see the guy's face because he wore a well-worn and frayed black ski mask.

37

THE MASKED MAN spoke like his voice was ruined from throat cancer. It was dark and rough, like a heavy smoker. Which I figured was fake.

He said, "Raise your hands! Turn around! Slow!"

I did as he asked. Raised my hands and turned, slowly.

He shoved me onto the deck of the boat.

"Lie down! Flat!"

I plopped down on the deck, landed my knees as loud as I could. I tried to make noise so Talbern and Marksy could hear me.

I had planned to slam the palms of my hands on the deck, but before I could, I felt a sharp, blunt pain in my back. The masked man had kicked me.

I turned my head to look through the window leading below deck.

I saw the flashlight beams moving around still. They hadn't heard a thing.

Lightning crackled again in the distance.

I saw in the glass's reflection that the masked man was about to kill me.

He stood above me. He pointed the shotgun at the back of my head. He stayed there like he was waiting for something. And he was.

Lightning whipped and cracked again, and thunder rolled, loud. The flash of lightning rippled across the sky. The sounds of the thunderclap echoed across the sky.

However, I didn't hear any of it because just then, the masked man used the loud sounds to drown out the sound of the shotgun blast.

He fired the shotgun right into the back of my head.

And everything went to black.

38

I HAD BEEN SHOT BEFORE.

I had three scars on my back from being shot. They looked worse than they were. I had been wearing Kevlar when I was shot in the back. But the bullets pierced through enough to leave me with three wicked scars.

I knew what a bullet felt like. I had never been shot by a slug from a shotgun or birdshot or a magnum round. And luckily, I still have not.

The round that shot me in the back of the head wasn't any of those.

I had been shot by a rubber bullet once. That hurt all kinds of serious pain.

This was similar, but it wasn't a rubber bullet either. A rubber bullet at that close range, back of the head. I might've been killed pretty easily.

The masked man had shot me with a beanbag round.

I woke up with the worst headache I had ever had. And I knew I was bleeding because I was lying in a pool of blood. I could taste it. I assumed it was mine because of the pain. And there was a long streak from a blood trail leading from me, up a tile floor I had never seen before, and it led up a small staircase.

At first, I thought that my head was pounding, but another minute went by, and I realized it wasn't my head. I was below deck on the Dayard sailboat. I knew that because the rocking was the boat.

My vision wasn't blurry like you would think. But it was not perfect twenty-twenty vision either.

My head hurt worse, if that was possible.

I realized that I might have a concussion or worse. I didn't have time to think about the worse part.

I tried to look around slowly. Then, I realized that even though my eyes were fine, my hearing wasn't.

I heard something, but it was muffled. Everything sounded underwater. I probably had two busted eardrums. I probably had blood seeping out of my ears.

I tried to raise my head. Then I realized my nose was bleeding. It wasn't broken, but when the beanbag slugged me in the back of the head, my face slammed into the deck, hard. I dropped my forehead, let it rest on the tile.

That damn rocking was driving me nuts. I could feel my brain slamming into my skull.

Everything hurt.

I tried breathing. I concentrated on that and nothing else for a long moment.

Then I heard the muffled sounds again.

There was movement off to my right.

I waited there for another long moment. I tried to breathe and not worry about anything else.

Finally, I rolled over onto my back.

I saw the masked man. He had his back turned to me.

He was holding someone up with his hand. I couldn't see what he was doing to her.

Talbern, I thought.

I tried to move. Tried to get up.

I couldn't!

Everything hurt!

I felt my hair. It was wet, which I figured was from the blood. Then I smelled something. My sense of smell must've been returning because the smell was faint at first. And then it got stronger.

I smelled gasoline.

I craned my head and looked down at the floor. It was covered in gas.

I looked back at the masked man.

He had tied Talbern and Marksy to two wooden chairs at a small breakfast nook. He held something over his head.

My vision blurred, no, not blurred. It was the rocking of the boat. I couldn't quite focus.

I looked again.

The masked man held up a plastic red can over his head. He was dumping the contents out over the women.

It was gas.

I tried to get up. I tried to push myself up. But my head hurt. I tried to sit up. I made it halfway. Then I felt a rush of blood to my head, and I felt feverish. Then I fell back.

Everything went black—again.

39

THERE WAS a question that I had wanted to ask Marksy. I wanted to ask her if she put the witness up to pointing the finger at James Dayard.

Part of me wondered if she had seen John mistaking him for his brother.

It was apparent now that she had. Either way, that question was no longer important. But that was the first thing that I thought of when I awoke the second time.

I had no idea how much time had passed since I blacked out again.

But I knew that something awful was happening because I woke up to someone screaming. It was a gut-wrenching scream, the kind that I haven't heard since the last time I was on a mission with the SEALs in the Middle East. The exact mission and the time in my life I couldn't remember.

The screaming rang out and echoed through the cabin like a fire alarm sounding.

I was staring at the roof of the cabin. And the first thing that I noticed was that we were no longer in darkness. The cabin was lit up in bright orange and red light.

Then, I smelled it.

The air was full of smells of gasoline and charred meat.

Suddenly, I felt adrenaline burst through me. I rolled over to my side and pushed myself up. I got on my knees.

I turned to look. I saw Talbern was crying and screaming at the top of her lungs. The masked man stood back, away from the table.

They were both staring at Marksy.

FBI Agent Marksy was on fire. She was blazing.

The masked man had set her ablaze and was now standing back and watching.

I looked at Marksy. She was still alive. She was shaking and dancing violently against her restraints, trying to free herself and trying to run to the water. But she couldn't move.

I couldn't see her face, but I knew it was in there somewhere.

My head continued to hurt—*no time for that*.

I jumped to my feet, almost falling right back down.

The masked man didn't hear me. He was staring on at the flaming FBI agent in what looked like a state of ecstasy.

I tried to rush him. But my feet didn't cooperate with the commands from my brain.

I fumbled into the kitchen counter, knocking over objects that I couldn't identify. Not then.

I put my left hand on something, and I was certain that it was a bag filled with bones. I stopped and stared at it. I couldn't take my mind off it for a moment. I was sure they were human bones.

Suddenly, Talbern screamed at me.

"WIDOW! LOOK OUT!"

I stumbled backward, not out of a reflex to her warning, just out of sheer luck.

There was a loud gunshot. And then another. And

another. And another. Four gunshots *boomed* and echoed into the cabin. The masked man fired at me. He missed each time. Partially, it was blind luck on my part. Partially, it was because the boat rocked. And partially it was because I kept fumbling all over the place. Being half-clumsy and half-unco-ordinated saved my life.

Smoke filled the air.

I stumbled again and fell back on my ass. I stared up at the masked man. He was firing at me with his SIG SAUER.

My vision returned to around ninety percent, and I saw his eyes. He aimed at me. He had me dead to rights, but he hesitated.

I waited. I was sure that he was going to shoot me dead right there. But he didn't.

I looked down at my hand. It was wet again.

The gasoline. He didn't want to shoot at it.

I looked back up at him. He stuffed the gun back into his waistband.

He reached behind him and slid a carpenter hammer out from nowhere. It must've been stuffed into the back of his pants.

I stared at the end. It was clean but dark. Like it had seen a life of bludgeoning those women, and it was ready for another use.

I pulled myself up to my feet.

Talbern was still screaming.

Marksy had completely stopped moving. But the flames were sparking and dancing and shooting off toward the breakfast table.

We had little time. The flames would spark far enough to hit the gas on the floor, or hit Talbern, who knew it.

She pushed with her feet and scooted as far back to the wall as she could.

I saw the shotgun. It was tossed on the bed, across from Talbern. But I had no chance of reaching it.

The masked man stood between Talbern and me and the shotgun.

"I hope you're ready to die, Widow!" he spoke, still using that raspy voice.

The masked man ran at me, hammer out. He looked like a madman, like an apparition from out of a nightmare.

I needed a weapon. I knew it.

Behind me was a kitchen. Maybe I could've found a kitchen knife or grabbed a frying pan.

I didn't do any of that.

I slammed my hand into my front pocket, grabbed the head of the toothbrush I swiped from the hotel, and jerked it out of my pocket.

Dizzily, I half sidestepped, and half slid to my right.

The masked man swung down with the hammer. It swung and barely missed my left shoulder.

I wrenched my elbow back as far and as fast as I could. I jabbed forward with full force, and I stabbed the handle of my toothbrush right through the masked man's neck, left side.

I pushed it all the way to the hilt.

Blood rushed out like water spraying out of a fire hydrant.

The masked man went straight down like a ton of bricks. He dropped the hammer, and a lighter slid out of his pocket.

He grabbed his neck wound and wrapped his fingers around the toothbrush. He jerked it out and screamed. Only no one could hear his scream because his voice box was severed or busted.

I could barely hear him because of my eardrums. Plus, Talbern was still screaming at the top of her lungs.

The masked man scrambled and snaked around on the

floor like he was dying a million agonizing deaths, which made me smile.

I left him and scrambled over to Talbern.

"Hurry, Widow! Hurry!"

"Hold still," I said.

I looked at her restraints. She was ziptied. Not a big deal. I scrambled back to the kitchen and found that knife I had thought of earlier. I went back to her and cut her free.

She ran from the smoldering dead body of the woman that she had once known and picked up her Glock from out of the kitchen sink.

The masked man must've thrown it in there. I hadn't even seen it.

She picked up Marksy's as well and tossed it to me.

She turned and pointed it at the masked man. She was going to shoot him.

"No!" I shouted partially because I still couldn't hear very well.

"Why not?"

"Let him suffer."

I ran to her and took her hand. I pulled her nearly off her feet and led her up the stairs and onto the deck. We scrambled off the boat.

We turned and watched the lower deck filled with orange and red fire. Suddenly, a huge fireball erupted and tore a hole in the roof.

Talbern stood there and watched.

I held onto her, tight until my adrenaline wore off. Then I leaned on her for a long moment as we watched the Dayards' sailboat burn.

After another moment, I dropped to my knees and then fell flat on my face.

I blacked out for the third time.

I HEARD A BUZZING SOUND.

I woke up in a place that I didn't know but recognized immediately. I was in a hospital room.

I wore the white gown, and the ID bracelet, and the IV drip—the whole nine yards.

I looked around and saw that the room was empty. There was another bed next to mine. But it was empty.

My vision had come back, which was good news.

My hearing was better, but the buzzing was annoying. Still, I could hear sounds. It was just like having bees live in my ears.

I saw my clothes were draped over the back of a chair. My shoes were on the floor. The hospital staff had even left Marksy's Glock in my pants pocket. I saw the bulge.

They must've thought I was an FBI agent like Talbern.

Where was Talbern?

I looked near my hand and found one of those call buttons. I pressed it twice. And a doctor showed up, instead of a nurse.

She wore a white lab coat instead of scrubs. She was

younger than me, shorter than Talbern, and had short brown hair.

She wore obvious contacts. They were bright blue.

She said, "Mr. Widow. How are you feeling?"

"Where's Talbern?"

"She's fine. But let's talk about you," she said. She walked to the end of the bed, and picked up my chart, looked at it. She flipped a page, looked over whatever information was there, and then flipped it back.

I said, "My hearing's not great. I hear buzzing. I feel like I busted my eardrums?"

"No. They're not busted. Just overly sensitive right now. I suggest not going to any nightclubs soon."

I nodded, reached down, and pressed a button on a remote that controlled the bed. I sat up as far as I could in it.

"Now, I want to talk about your head. You got hit pretty hard with something. Looks like a baseball."

"It was a beanbag round from a shotgun."

She nodded like that was what she expected me to say.

I asked, "What's the damage? Concussion?"

"That's the strange thing. The force of the blow and the impact of the beanbag must've been very hard."

She paused there and scooped out an X-ray that was stuffed in an envelope on the chart. She walked over to a table lamp near the bathroom door. She flipped it on and tilted the shade so that there was a lot of light coming out.

She held the X-ray up to it.

"This is an X-ray of your skull we took while you were out."

I stayed quiet.

"The beanbag hit your skull with enough force to cause a major concussion and even brain damage."

"I got brain damage?"

"No. That's what I'm saying. Normally, that's probably what would've happened. But see how your skull has all these signs of older abrasions?"

She pointed at all these older-looking shadow areas on my skull.

"I guess."

"Those are signs of injuries that happened in the past. They healed, but they changed the circumference of your skull. See, human bones don't heal in a perfect, smooth way. They scar kind of like skin, in a way."

"So?"

"When the bone heals, it usually heals to be rugged and thicker, like building up calluses."

"What does that mean?"

"It means that your skull is thicker than most people because you've had a lot of injuries. If I had to guess I'd say either you've spent your life as a professional motorcycle dare-devil who has never worn his helmet or you hold the world title for a heavyweight boxer because you've been hit in the head—a lot."

"Am I going to be okay?"

"Just don't go getting hit in the head soon. Got it?"

I nodded.

"I want you to take it easy and rest for at least two more days."

I asked, "More days? How long have I been here?"

"You've been asleep for two whole days."

"Two days?"

"Yeah. That's why your FBI friends are gone. They went home."

I nodded, watched her walk to the door. She stopped and turned back to me.

"You have some stitches back there. If you feel any

discomfort when you lie down, turn on your side."

I nodded again, and she left.

I turned and picked up a telephone that was next to the bed. I got a prerecorded voice for the hospital's internal network. I dialed nine, which got me an outside line like it almost always does.

Then I froze. What number was I going to dial?

I tried to remember Talbern's number, but I don't think she ever gave it to me.

I hung it up.

My first thought was to get dressed and get out of there. Maybe if I got to a computer, I could look up the FBI number in New York.

Then I remembered I had a card from Clayton. I moved my legs and swung them out and got up out of bed.

I felt okay, just a little slow.

I walked over to my pants and sifted through the pockets. I found my passport and bank card and the business card from Clayton.

I went back to the bed, sat down, and dialed the number.

It rang and rang. I almost gave up when a voice answered.

"Hello?"

"Clayton?"

"Yeah, who is this?"

"It's Jack Widow."

Silence.

"What can I do for you?"

"I'm in the hospital in Portland. I woke up here. Apparently, I slept for two days."

"Yes," Clayton said.

"Can you tell me what happened? No one is here from the FBI."

Silence again. I heard voices in the background.

Clayton said, "You guys found the killer. Apparently, John, Jr.'s body was discovered at Mr. Dayard's boat, which you blew up."

"What about the FBI agents?"

I heard more voices. It sounded like a celebration.

Clayton said, "Yeah. One of them was okay. The other died. I'm sorry."

"What about James?"

"That's good news. He's out."

I paused, looked up at the door to the hallway.

"He's out?" I asked. "That quick?"

"Yeah, well, we found a judge that granted him a stay of execution, and because of the evidence that his brother wasn't dead, they granted him bail until a new trial could be set. But we feel he'll get acquitted."

"Well, that's good news. Congratulations."

"Yeah, thanks. We couldn't have done it without you. The secretary would love to thank you personally, but he's spending the evening with his son."

"He's there?"

"Yeah. John just got here a few hours ago."

I paused a beat.

"Widow?"

"John?"

"What?" Clayton asked.

"You said, John."

"I meant James. A slip of the tongue. A lot going on here tonight. Can I help you with anything else?"

"No. I guess not."

"Okay. Have a good one," Clayton said, and he hung up. The line went dead.

I hung up the phone and stood up off the bed. I went to

the bathroom, opened the door, and stared at myself in the mirror.

I looked like a man who slept for decades. I had some serious bedhead and stubble on my face.

I ran the water and cleaned my face, turned off the faucet.

Clayton had said, John. I thought about the Dayard family home again.

Why did Dayard need all that security?

My animal brain wouldn't let it go.

Then it hit me. John Jr., a part of me, had thought that the security wasn't for the secretary, but was really to protect John Jr. I had thought that maybe they were hiding him. But the guys that I had seen weren't just there to protect the secretary. They were there to do what he said. They weren't sentries. They were mercenaries.

I closed my eyes, tried to remember the boat. There was that black car in the parking lot. And the masked man. And his guns. He had Secret Service weapons. The Remington 870 and the SIG SAUER were both used by the Service.

And the bones. They found John Jr.'s body, Clayton had told him.

I remember there were human bones on the kitchen counter.

Secretary Dayard wanted me to help his son. He flew me out there and gave me that whole story about the prodigal son who was a failure. He told me about the suicide. Painted that picture of how he was just a dying old man surrounded by photographs of a family he had lost.

The Dayards were evil. Father and son.

I needed Talbern.

I got dressed and ditched the hospital gown and ID and the IV.

As I was putting on my shoes, the phone rang.

"Hello?"

"Widow. It's Pawn," a voice said. I recognized it, but there was something wrong. Something was off.

"Yeah," I said.

"I'm glad that you're feeling better."

"Yeah," I said. I was tying my shoes at the same time.

"Listen, we have a little problem."

"What's up?"

"Well, look, I know that you and Talbern have grown close over the last couple of days."

I didn't like where this was going.

"I know she's done a great job. You both have."

"Okay," I said. I was confused.

"She deserves to take a little sabbatical. I've got no problem with that."

I stayed quiet.

"Listen, you don't have to put her on the phone. I just wanted you to tell her she can take as long as she wants. Tell her to call me when she's ready to come back to work. You both did a good job, Widow."

I froze. I felt my skin crawl.

Pawn didn't know where she was. He thought Talbern was with me.

He asked, "She is with you, right? She left here yesterday and said she was going back to wait for you to wake up."

I thought for a moment. Talbern had left the FBI and come back to Portland to wait for me to wake up. He said that she had left yesterday. Therefore, she would be here already.

Dayard had her. James had eyeballed her at the prison. He took her. Had to be. Maybe he had wanted to kill Marksy, but one of his father's guys beat him to it. The masked man wasn't Clayton, that was obvious, but he had been one of his guys.

"Widow?" Pawn asked.

I couldn't tell him. I couldn't tell him because Dayard had eyes and ears in the bureau. Plus, I didn't want FBI red tape.

"Yeah. I gotta go," I said, and I hung up the phone.

I pulled Marksy's Glock out of my pocket. I ejected the magazine and checked it.

I dry fired the weapon. It worked as advertised.

I slipped the magazine back in and chambered a round.

I had only been to Dayard's house by air, but I knew where it was. It was less than an hour out of the city, in the hills and on the coast.

Now I needed a ride.

41

THE THING ABOUT POLICE DEPARTMENTS, especially for major cities, was that they are operated by two opposing forces. The first is to maintain law and order, which means solving and preventing crimes. It means going to nine-one-one calls. It means risking life and taxpayer property to keep the peace.

The second thing that runs a city police department is the budget.

Police departments across the country were all facing tight budgets. I read that in newspapers across the nation.

Places like hospitals caused these two forces to clash because hospitals were natural targets for crime. But anything hardly ever happens at a hospital to cause the need for police to be present. So what do most police departments do to make people think they are present?

They park their police cruisers out front or near the emergency room. They want people to see them.

I walked out to the parking lot of the hospital, passing nurses and staff who barely gave me a second glance.

I walked around the parking lot for less than two minutes

before I found a parked Portland police cruiser. When I saw it, I smiled because I was banking on the budgetary constraints, stopping the police from parking one of their newer models. And they hadn't.

Parked out front was an older model Dodge Charger. It was all black, which I had no problem with.

Hopefully, they didn't have any antitheft software installed. And even if they did, it would be a long time before they realized it was stolen.

I looked around the parking lot and saw no one. There was no one watching.

I took out the Glock and reversed it in my hand. I half swung it to the window to break it, but then I stopped.

Instead of breaking the window, I tried the handle first. It wasn't locked.

Then I thought, why would it be? They didn't expect someone to steal it.

I opened the door, dumped myself down onto the driver's seat. I reached down and racked the seat all the way back, pulled my feet in, and shut the door.

I tossed the Glock on the seat next to me, and I reached down, pulled the ignition column off, and tried to remember how the hell to hot-wire a car. It had been a while.

I tore open some wires that seemed right, and I clicked them together. Nothing happened. I tried a different wire, and they sparked, and the engine roared to life.

I gassed it and tied the wires together.

Sometimes you just get lucky, I thought. Then I thought about Talbern, and I thought about Karen Dekker, and I thought about Marksy.

I reversed the Charger and flipped the headlamps on. I drove out of the parking lot, followed the signs to the interstate, and headed north.

42

I drove nearly an hour, following the winding interstate north. I basically drove by a vague sense of where the Dayard house had been located. I knew it was on a dark coastline and it wasn't far from Portland.

Luckily, the skies were clear, and the stars were out.

I drove until I saw a sign for a wealthy-sounding community called Trident Coast. There was an advertisement for new homes coming soon on a billboard close to the interstate. That had to be it. The land looked dark and rural, yet wealthy.

I drove onto an off-ramp and followed signs that pointed to a beach.

I followed the main road and curved around numerous bends until I saw what I was looking for. The trees thinned, and I saw the skyline. It was identical to the skyline I remembered over the Dayard house.

It was here somewhere.

I slowed the car and tried to imagine what I had seen the other night from the helicopter.

I remembered much of the topography. I drove until I saw

houses that looked similar. They were far apart and old and Victorian. There were long drives and high fences.

I drove until I came to the end of the street. There was one drive at the end. I couldn't see the house, but I knew it was the right one.

I knew because there was a high brick wall with a security camera on the gate. And I saw floodlights mounted on the tops of the walls. This was the right place, or it was a high-security prison.

I rolled the car up to the end of the road, which led down to a private beach. And then I saw the water. The Atlantic Ocean was beautiful in the moonlight.

I left the engine running because if I killed it; I wasn't sure that I could hot-wire it again. But I killed the lights.

I left the car in park and got out, took the Glock with me.

I tucked it into my front pocket and reached back down into the car and popped the trunk. I figured that the cops probably wouldn't leave weapons or live ammunition in the trunk, but there might be something valuable in there.

I shut the door, walked back to the trunk, and lifted it.

The sounds of low crashing waves washed up from the beach.

A small light flashed on and lit up the trunk. I sifted through it. It was one of the more cluttered police trunks I had ever seen. I found a lot of basic equipment, like traffic cones and road flares. No shotgun. No ammunition. No weapons of any kind.

I found two items that I could use. One was a small Maglite, which isn't actually small; it was just the smaller size. I left it.

The second thing was a cheap-looking police bulletproof vest.

It was dark blue and had the word: *POLICE* written on the front in huge white font.

I inspected it. It looked worn but never used as in it had no bullet holes in it.

I slipped it on. It fit well enough and gave me a slight advantage. I doubted that Dayard's men wore vests.

I shut the trunk and looked at the gate. I wasn't getting in that way. I ran down to the beach.

The wall was high, but not impossible to climb. I ran down the length of it for a good five minutes until the beach ran out, and there was nothing left but the ocean and the edge of the Dayard's property.

The wall stopped there because there was no more need for it. If I wanted to go any farther, then I would have to swim. But now I could see the house. I saw the back of it and the huge garden and the helicopter pad.

The chopper was there. It was parked under white spotlights.

I crouched down and scanned the property. I still heard the buzzing in my ears; only now it was more like a ringing. But my eyes worked fine.

I saw no sign of anyone outside. There were lights on in the house.

I stepped back to the wall and jumped up, grabbed the top ledge, and pulled myself over.

I landed on the other side and smiled. I smiled because I realized I was grateful the Dayards didn't have any dogs. Then I wondered why they didn't?

I wasn't sure about the lights they had placed everywhere. They probably had some lights that were motion-sensor. I stayed low and took it slow and steady.

It took me a while to make it close to the house.

As I neared the back door, I slowed and took out the

Glock. I pointed it downward; I didn't want to shoot the wrong person. I looked around and saw no one.

I ran to the back door and put my back to the wall next to it.

The back door was mostly glass. I edged to the side of the door and peeked in. No one was standing there. Then I heard a sound. Footsteps. But not from inside the door. It was from the other side of the house from me. I ran straight and out and ducked down near the helicopter. I waited.

I saw it was the guy who rode with us the other night—one of Clayton's guys.

He stopped on the side of the house. He was smoking a cigarette.

He smoked it and flicked it out on the grass. He turned and walked back the way he had come.

I jumped up and ran after him. I slowed my pace as I neared the corner. I peeked around it. He was meandering.

I crept up close behind him, as close as I was comfortable with. Then I ran faster, and he heard me. He turned around fast.

I flipped the Glock in my hand and used the side of it as a knuckleduster. I punched him square in the face. I heard the bones in his nose crack. He went back off his feet like a puppet with the strings cut.

I jumped on top of him before he could scream out. I kneed him right in the chest, just above the solar plexus, took the breath out of him. He held onto his nose with both hands. Blood gushed out of it.

I pushed the Glock into his neck.

He felt it. He looked at me with horror in his eyes.

I asked, "How many of Clayton's guys are inside?"

He said nothing.

I used my left hand and punched him square on the back

of his hands, crushing them into his broken nose. He screamed as loud as a man with no air could scream, which wasn't loud at all.

"How many? I won't ask again."

"Three. And me."

I nodded. That was what I had thought. The other night, Clayton had picked us up with a driver, and then there were the three other guys, counting this one. Five in total. He had a crew of five, counting Clayton. But they were short a man. One of them was dead, the one who had been scoping the sailboat in the car, waiting for us to play along. He wore the mask, pretended to be the dead son, and ambushed us.

But he was dead now. That left the four of them remaining.

Three were in the house and him. That equals five in total.

"Don't kill me," he said.

"Which one of you killed Karen Dekker?"

"What?"

"Was it you?"

"No. No. That was Clayton. All Clayton."

I came down close to him.

I said, "But you knew about it, right?"

He said nothing.

I came back up and pointed the Glock in his face. He stayed still.

I stood up off him. And then as fast as I could, I dropped a knee down on him—hard as I could. This time I didn't land on his chest. I landed on his throat, crushing his larynx.

I got up and watched him squirm around, gasping for air that wouldn't come.

He was dead in less than a minute.

I searched his pockets and found nothing of interest

except for his weapon. Another SIG Sauer. I took it, and unloaded it, dry fired it like I did the Glock. It worked. I reloaded the magazine and chambered it as well.

I left the dead former Secret Service agent there.

I stood up. The ringing in my ears was still there. My vision was still okay. And I didn't feel bad, but when I stood up, I felt lightheaded.

Not now, I thought.

In the SEALs teams, if this had been a mission, I would've had backup and state-of-the-art equipment and intel and a plan.

I had no plan. My plan was to kill them all.

I continued to go straight in the direction the dead guy was going. I walked past windows with lights on, but I saw no movement in them.

I heard music playing from the second floor.

I ended up coming around the house to the front. I stopped at the driveway. No one was out front, but there was a garage, and the door was open.

I peered in. Saw a black car, like the one I saw at the harbor, but not the same one because the driver of that car was dead.

I walked into the garage. There was a door that led into the house. I almost opened it, but I stopped and stepped back.

There was a long workbench with tools laid out above it.

I saw each tool had a designated place or hook to hang on with an outline of the tool. I noticed a hammer was missing. It must've been the one the masked man had with him.

There was no other hammer, but there was a crowbar. It was a black steel thing, with fine craftsmanship spent making it. I knew quality when I saw it. And this was a fine tool.

I smiled because I needed a melee weapon. I couldn't just

start picking off the rest of his crew with bullets. Gunshots make a lot of noise. Crowbars are quieter.

I slipped the crowbar off its hook and felt it in my hand. It was lightweight, but hard.

I took it in my left hand and held the Glock in my right.

The door led to the pantry. I passed through it, slowly, and walked into the kitchen, where I found the male nurse, whose name I had forgotten.

He was trying to put one half of a sandwich in his mouth when he saw me. Instead, he froze.

To be honest, I wasn't sure where to categorize him. I doubted he had anything to do with the crimes that this house had committed. He wasn't innocent. Being an accessory is still a crime.

I had to take him out. But I didn't have to kill him. I walked up to him, pointed the Glock at him. He didn't say a word. He dropped the sandwich. It fell to the floor.

I stuck the gun in his face and asked, "Where are the car keys?"

He said nothing, but pointed to a drawer under the countertop.

I put the crowbar on the table in front of him and reached down and bunched up the collar of his shirt. I pulled him to his feet and dragged him over to the drawer.

"Get them."

He slid open the drawer and pulled the keys out.

I checked down the hallway and then pulled him back through the pantry into the garage.

"Pop the trunk," I commanded.

He pressed a button on the key, and the trunk popped open.

I dragged him over to it and said, "Get in."

He got in.

"Keys?" I asked with my free hand open.

He put the keys in my palm.

"Cellphone," I commanded.

He didn't argue. He pulled his phone out of his pocket and handed it to me.

"Keep quiet."

He nodded.

I slammed the trunk shut and locked the car. I tossed the phone and the keys onto the workbench. I figured the cops would find him. I wasn't concerned with him identifying me, not then. All that was on my mind was Talbern.

I went back into the kitchen and picked up the crowbar and continued down the hall.

I searched the bottom floor and found no one. There was nothing but huge, empty rooms.

I turned and walked up the stairs to the top floor. I heard laughing and music.

First, I checked all the rooms on my way to the source of the music. They were all empty.

The room with the music and voices was Dayard's bedroom.

I walked to it and heard footsteps. I backed up and waited.

One guard walked out. It was one of Clayton's guys. He was on the helicopter with us.

He stopped outside the door on his way to the bathroom. He froze and stared right at me.

I cracked him in the face as hard as I could with the crowbar. He dropped like a ton of bricks. Blood gushed out a gaping wound that was left on his forehead.

He was probably dead. I wasn't sure.

Then I heard Clayton's voice from the bedroom.

"Sanson, you out there? What the hell was that?"

No more sneaking around, I thought.

I burst through the open doorway.

The room was the same as it had been the other night, only now it was full of energy and life. It almost seemed like a different place.

The secretary sat in his chair, only now he was wearing a suit without a tie. Sitting across from him, where I had sat, was his son. He wore a shirt and tie, no jacket.

Clayton stood in the center of the room, facing me, and holding a brandy snifter. The last one of his guys leaned against the fireplace, smoking a cigar.

Then I noticed that so were both Dayards. They had cigars hanging from their fingers.

A CD player was playing old soft rock music over a big loudspeaker. The song I didn't recognize, but it was something somber and probably from the nineteen fifties.

Then there was Talbern. She was in the same seat that she had been in a couple of nights ago. Her hands were tightly duct-taped out in front of her. She had a black ballgag stuffed in her mouth, with a black leather contraption strapped around her head.

She was fully clothed, but she was missing her shoulder rig and her jacket. She had a torn-up top and trousers. She wore no shoes.

Her face wasn't beaten, but she had tears streaming down her face. She looked terrified.

Clayton stayed standing, but he moved his hand down to his gun, which was under his suit jacket. I saw it.

I glanced over at the other guy. He was wearing his, as well. I saw he was thinking about going for it. I saw it in his eyes.

Both Dayards had no guns. Their hands were visible.

I said, "Which one of you killed Karen Dekker?"

No answer. I kept the Glock pointed at Clayton. He didn't move.

I said, "Dayard, you were convincing. A sick old man. A military man. Like me. You read through my files. Did you get a psychological profile of me too?"

He was quiet.

"You gave me that bullshit about your family and your cancer, which might be real. Hell, I don't know. But then you laid it on thick about your sons."

I walked into the room more and dropped the crowbar.

"You knew that I'd pick up on John, Jr. You gave me that whole charade about losing your son. I doubt you even gave a shit about that one. I think he wasn't the only one with psychological problems. I'm sure you passed that psycho shit off to both of them. One son killed himself years ago, and the other one turns out to be a serial killer. Then he gets caught. So, you plant the seed that maybe it's not James. He's the good son. It was John. Only he's really dead.

"You get Clayton here to kill another girl, the same as the ones that James murdered just so the FBI would have to stop the execution."

Dayard said, "Widow, we can work this out. I have what I want. What do you want?"

I ignored him.

"How did you get Dekker to go along with it?" I asked Clayton.

He didn't speak.

"You only had a few days to save James from lethal injection, and you didn't have a woman who actually went AWOL. So, you had to have tricked her somehow to pretend to. I figure you promised Dekker money. She had just gotten orders she didn't want. She wanted out. So, you lured her out to the boat. She thought you were going to fake her death, but then you killed her. Is that right?"

Clayton said nothing.

"I figure she was your best candidate. You concocted this whole scenario where John, Jr. was out there, still alive, living on a boat somewhere. He traveled up to Florida and found Dekker. He killed her, setting this whole thing into motion. But you didn't count on me finding her dog tags. You planned for someone to find her body.

"But once you learned who I was, you manipulated me from the start."

Dayard said, "It's all water under the bridge now. Widow, don't do anything you'll regret."

I stayed quiet, kept my eyes on Clayton.

Dayard said, "Widow, I have money. I can make you a rich man. I have influence. You would be shocked at what power can get you in this world."

"Which one of you killed, Dekker?" I asked Clayton again.

He said, "Does it matter?"

I shrugged and shot him in his chest.

Clayton flew back off his feet. Blood splattered across the center of the room. It sprayed across Dayard's face.

The last of Clayton's guys went for his gun. I turned faster and squeezed the trigger of the Glock, twice.

Two bullets tore through his center mass. Red mist sprayed up into the air.

The guy flew forward and crashed on the coffee table in front of Talbern.

I turned the Glock to James Dayard.

He didn't move.

"Widow, no! Don't!" his father begged.

James Dayard spoke. He mumbled a word, but I had no

idea what. My ears weren't ringing anymore. They were buzzing hard. The Glock's gunshots were deafening to me. The doctor had told me to avoid loud noises.

I said, "Don't speak."

I shot him once, center mass. I heard his father scream and drop his drink and cigar. He leaped out of his chair and across to his son. He planted two hands on the hole that used to be James Dayard's chest.

For a guy with terminal cancer, he moved pretty fast.

I felt dizzy again.

I walked over to Talbern and grabbed the duct tape with my free hand, and ripped it off.

She did the rest of it and pulled out her ball gag. She tore the leather straps that held it on and dropped them to the floor.

She jumped up and hugged me tightly.

I held her back.

Dayard continued to hoot and holler. I ignored him and pulled Talbern away from the sofa and out to the hallway.

"Wait for me. Bottom of the stairs," I said, giving her the SIG Sauer.

She didn't argue, which I had expected.

I walked back into the room.

Gunsmoke filled the air.

"General," I called Dayard. He turned and looked at me.

He didn't speak, didn't call out.

I shot him in the head. He dropped back onto his son.

I slipped the Glock back into my pocket and bent over, picked up the crowbar, and wiped my fingerprints off it with the bottom of my shirt. I tossed it back to the ground.

I went back out and down the hall and the stairs.

Talbern grabbed me and hugged me tight again.

"I thought I was dead. I thought they were going to kill me."

"It's over now."

She didn't let go.

I held her for a long moment, and then I said, "Let's get the hell out of here."

She followed me back out of the house. We went through the backyard and back to the wall that I had leaped over.

I lifted her up and over, and then I followed. We ran down the beach, back to the police car.

"Where did you get this?"

"Don't ask."

I took the Glock and threw it into the water and told her to ditch the SIG Sauer.

"Why?" she asked.

"Talbern, we can't be here. I just killed a US secretary of defense."

She nodded and threw the gun after mine.

"What if they link my fingerprints in the house?"

"That's okay. We were here before. But we don't need to leave fingerprints on stolen guns."

"Have you done this before?" she asked.

I stayed quiet.

We got into the car and drove off.

I DIDN'T RETURN to the hospital.

We drove all night and the next day and most of that night until we ended up in Jacksonville, Florida.

I spent a couple of nights at Talbern's apartment, five nights, to be exact. She didn't go back to work, not yet. She had spoken on the phone with Pawn. He mentioned the guy in the trunk—a witness. He also mentioned that the guy couldn't remember who he had seen.

Something told me it was only after Pawn had convinced him to forget.

We lay in bed, naked. And we heard the rain pound on her windows.

She said, "You know what?"

"What?"

"We should go to Jamaica, like for real."

"How long are you going to stay away from work?"

"I don't know. I feel safe in your arms. I don't want to go back."

I thought about that for a long moment.

"What are you going to do?"

"What do you mean?" I asked her.

"Are you going to stick around?"

I wanted to lie to her. But I couldn't. I didn't like to lie to someone I cared about.

I said, "I don't stick around. I need to move."

"Wish I could go with you."

"You can do whatever you want."

She rolled over and faced me, ran her fingers over my chest.

"Do you want me to go with you?"

I thought for a moment. I told her the truth.

"I do."

She smiled and kissed me, and we did all the things that we had been doing for five days.

I stayed another day and night and morning. But by that afternoon, I was back on the road. Talbern returned to work. She had lots to do. She needed to debrief. And apparently, someone assassinated Dayard, killing all his men and his son.

The FBI thought it was a whole, well-trained wet work crew. They were most likely foreign. She said that it was a huge mess. And Pawn had asked for her specifically to come and help.

That last day Talbern dropped me off at a bus stop in Jacksonville.

I bought a ticket west.

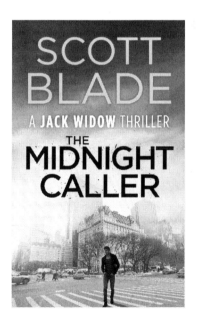

Out now!

THE MIDNIGHT CALLER: A BLURB

A midnight phone call.
A beautiful spy.
A nuclear threat and Jack Widow.

Former undercover NCIS Agent Jack Widow is in New York City for his birthday. He's living the good life. Not a care in the world. Not until his hotel phone rings at midnight.

A woman with a seductive Russian accent speaks, making a desperate plea for her life. She claims to need help. She claims that she's being held captive by a group of dangerous men.

Suddenly, the phone goes dead.

Who is she? Is her claim real?

Jack Widow must find out. No choice. He's not the kind of guy to do nothing. But the truth will drag him headfirst into a horrifying plot ripped right out of an international nightmare.

Readers are saying…

★★★★★ An action-packed spy thriller.

★★★★★ A thrilling, suspenseful, and engaging read!

CHAPTER 1

Joseph McConnell, "Jo Jo" to his friends, left the meeting thinking that the right thing to do was to go to the FBI. But they weren't his first choice. His first choice would have been to go to the NCIS. But how could he do that?

He did not know who to trust. The NCIS was risky. Homeland Security would be monitored. And the FBI?

He just didn't know. He needed time to think.

McConnell was a retired military officer himself. He had not retired with the highest rank for a man his age, but high enough. He was satisfied. Having low ambitions helped.

Never had he been anyone important. Nor had he ever aspired to be. He was happy in his former position. He had been satisfied with his accomplishments in the shadow of greater men.

There was nothing to be ashamed of. In the same breath, he also had nothing to be proud of either. Not really. He lived a mediocre life because he was a mediocre man.

At best, he deserved honorable mentions only for participation, not anything more.

Today, he lived a nice little life in the suburbs outside of

Norfolk, Virginia, a well-established neighborhood called Brampton Heights, with sprawling sections of trees, surrounding a mid-level golf course. It was quite the place to retire. Mostly, he had been able to retire there not because of his accomplishments in the Navy, but rather for his silence. He knew things, dark things. And he had been rewarded for keeping his mouth shut.

The thing he knew now that he had learned today was too much, even for him. It was a secret that he couldn't keep.

This neighborhood was far above his pay grade, above his class. Most of his neighbors were well-to-do CEOs, retired congressmen, law partners in international firms, or members of the military who outranked him. Six four-star generals lived there. Soon to be five, because one was on his deathbed, although he had been for six months. Cancer.

More importantly, to McConnell, there were two retired admirals. He knew them personally. He was proud to have a relationship with each man. They were friendly with him, not in the "come over for cigars and a glass of bourbon every week" kind of way, but casual enough to where he had gotten invites to their homes for big neighborhood parties.

If either admiral had been interrogated, he would have acknowledged that he knew McConnell. And neither would have an opinion of him, one way or the other. He knew that. He had no illusions about that. He was forgettable.

McConnell knew many Navy personnel. That had been his branch of the military.

Not in twenty years of service did he ever stray. Never had he ever betrayed his commander's trust. Even though McConnell's rank wasn't as high as he would have liked, it was still high enough for him to know things. Classified things. Bad things. Sometimes illegal things.

Under normal circumstances, some of the things he knew

would have made the most loyal dog bark. Whenever there had been a delicate mission in the past, he had been the guy to count on to oversee it, or at least to be a part of it.

Good Ole Jo Jo can keep a secret, they would say, or they would think. They must have because they trusted him with secrets—dirty, dirty secrets.

McConnell stepped out of his town car and shut the door. He left it parked in the driveway because he used the garage to house the ten-foot-by-ten-foot model of the maritime battle of Midway, which he had spent the last six months constructing and piecing together, painstakingly. Many of the pieces had to be specially crafted from a hobby and craft shop on the edge of town. And others had to be ordered off the internet.

Before the meeting that he'd just left, he had gone to the shop and picked up a final piece. It was a model depiction of two fighter planes going up against a Japanese plane.

The piece was still in the box, sealed with plastic wrap. He was eager to pull it out and rig it up to complete the model set.

McConnell did not know what to do about the subject of his meeting, but he did know that once he took out the set of planes and placed them in just the right place on his model set, he would be in a state of bliss. He could forget for a moment. He could ignore the danger that was coming.

McConnell closed the door to his town car and walked up the driveway. He left the vehicle doors unlocked. He hardly ever locked them because the car was controlled by one of those electric key locks, which he did not like to use. He preferred regular keys because he considered himself to be old-school. He liked pressing the lockdown, but he couldn't on this car because it just popped back up.

At his front door, McConnell paused and switched the

brown paper bag containing the airplane models from his right hand to his left. He used his right hand to unlock the front door and push it open. He entered the house.

The outside light switched on automatically at about the same moment.

The house was completely dark except for a lamp that his wife had turned on before she left.

She was out with her friends, probably playing bridge, or mahjong, or some other game where she could lose his money. At least that was the common excuse that she gave him. Like he cared, he didn't. He always pretended to care about where she was and what she was doing to feign interest, usually in front of the grandchildren. The truth was he couldn't care less. She could leave and never return, and he would find a way to live with himself. Of that, he was sure.

Luckily, he did not have to pretend too often since their two kids were adults who had children of their own and lived in faraway states.

Suddenly, he wondered if that's why they had called him to the meeting. More than his reputation for being trustworthy, and the fact that they needed him to set up contact with the Russian captain in the first place, the other thing was that he had no family here to worry about.

He did not have to worry about what they were planning. He did not have to worry about his family members being in danger. When the time came and the event that they were planning occurred, he could fly out to Colorado and see his son. He could be far away from the radius of damage that was on its way.

McConnell was all for returning to a better time. That's ultimately what the men in his meeting wanted. They were patriots, and they wanted to return to when the military meant something when honor was still alive and well, when they had a clear-cut enemy unlike now, where the enemy was not a state with a flag.

In the meeting, the Listener had explained to him their plans. The Listener explained everything. And as with his wife, McConnell feigned that he was calm and collected, that he could be trusted, but on the inside, he was terrified about what the Listener proposed—terrified.

But he listened and nodded and went along with it all. He acted like he understood, which he did. He was ashamed of the state of today's military.

Today's Navy had invisible enemies, unlike thirty years ago when times had more honor. Back then, they had Russia. They had the Cold War. They knew who their enemy was.

Politicians today used the Navy for spying and intel gathering like it was a spy satellite. And those pinheads at the NSA did not respect what the Navy was for. They did not respect the firepower that the Navy had.

What was the Navy doing with all their firepower now? Training exercises. Today's sailors and marines and SEALs hardly got much action. All they ever did was pretend.

It was all hogwash to McConnell and the Listener and the other. A disgrace.

To McConnell and the men in his meeting, the Navy wasn't a library or a tool for spying. It was a broadsword. It wasn't the transportation system that it had become for other branches to sail across seas. The Navy had the nukes. The Navy was the US military's atomic weapon. The Navy was the game-changer.

And now it was all being squandered.

Even though McConnell could agree with the sentiments of the small group of men that he had been speaking with, he wasn't sure about their plan.

He tossed his keys on the bar top in his kitchen and set

down the bag with the models inside, carefully. He shivered a bit because the house was colder than usual.

Probably that time of year, he thought.

He opened the fridge and looked in. He cursed under his breath because his wife had thrown out the leftovers and had cooked nothing for him. Sure, there was food, but it was her duty to cook it, not his. That was how he was raised.

That was another reason why he was glad she was out of the house all the time. She had abandoned tradition long ago, the moment the youngest kid was gone.

They were living separate lives. They were roommates more than anything else. She had her room upstairs, and he had his downstairs, which suited him just fine.

It had all started with different drawers in a dresser and then separate closets and then different bathrooms. Before too long, she had taken over the entire second floor of the house, and he was evicted from it.

McConnell closed the refrigerator, went over to a cabinet on the opposite side of the kitchen, and took out a rocks glass. He wanted a snifter, but the only two he had were dirty, still in the sink. Another wifely duty being ignored, in his opinion.

He settled for a clean rocks glass and opened another cabinet above the bar and stovetop. It held a host of different liquor bottles. All dark. All whiskey or bourbon or a blend of the two or cognac, which was his favorite. He only took out the whiskey for special occasions when he wanted to get completely hammered.

He poured the cognac and swished it around in the glass. A strong scent floated out and caressed his sense of smell. He smiled, set the open bottle down on the bar top, and took a sip. Not bad.

He walked to a side door that led to the garage, scooped

up the bag with the model planes, and took it with him on his way through the door.

The garage was dark and colder than the inside of the house, but only by a degree or two.

He walked in, leaving the side door open so that a pool of light crept in, enough to illuminate his path.

He set the bag down near the table with the model battle scene and turned to switch on the light. He flipped it, and the overhead light flicked on. The light was a single fixture with two bright bulbs. It didn't matter to him that the light wasn't enough to light up every nook and cranny of the garage. It worked perfectly as a spotlight on the table. Plus, he liked the atmosphere that the lower lighting created. It made the whole room feel like one of those cigar-smoking rooms you see in old movies.

The model table, itself, was lit perfectly. Shadows crept out and away from the pieces in just the right way.

On the edge of the model table was a glass ashtray, which McConnell was proud of because he had stolen it from the USS Missouri, which he had been stationed on during Desert Storm. Famously, it was the first battleship to launch Tomahawks into Iraqi-held enemy territory. He was always proud of that fact, even though he had had absolutely nothing to do with it.

There was a half-smoked cigar resting on the ashtray next to a gold-plated lighter. It was his cigar. He had put it out the night before and saved it.

McConnell stood over the model table and smiled. He was about to complete another masterpiece.

Most of his fellow retired sailors could look back on their careers with great pride. McConnell was only content with his. But creating these models was something he was proud of.

It was sad to think that this was more of his life's work than his military record.

Still, there was one final piece to the puzzle.

He turned, still swallowing cognac, and returned to pick up the model pieces. That's when he came face to face with the man in black and the business end of a silenced SIG Sauer.

The man in black had a name, but McConnell did not know it. He only knew who he was by reputation. The first time that he'd ever met the guy was over an hour ago at the meeting.

Even then, the man in black was silent.

Now he spoke. His voice was subtle and eerily normal, which was almost more frightening than the gun, strangely. Maybe it was the calmness in it. Or maybe it was the lack of humanity in it.

The man in black asked, "Where's your wife?"

McConnell did not put his hands up to show surrender. He did not drop his glass of cognac. He just stayed there, still, and said, "She's out."

"When is she coming back?"

McConnell shrugged.

"Where are your children?"

Without hesitation, he said, "They moved out years ago."

The man in black nodded. He believed him.

Just then, he asked a question that sent fear straight to McConnell's bones. It was the fear you feel the moment you know that you're going to die.

The man in black asked, "She know about what we're doing?"

A WORD FROM SCOTT

Thank you for reading NAME NOT GIVEN. You got this far—I'm guessing that you enjoyed Widow.

The story continues in a fast-paced series that takes Widow (and you) all around the world, solving crimes, righting wrongs.

If you love Tom Clancy, then THE MIDNIGHT CALLER the next book in this series must be your next read. This one has Jack Widow in a NYC hotel, when the phone rings from an internal line at midnight. A woman with a Russian accent pleads for his help. Saving her will propel Widow into an international conspiracy with Russian spies, American conspirators, and a missing nuclear submarine.

Sometimes, a purging fire is necessary to destroy the past. This is how FIRE WATCH starts for Molly DeGorne who is standing in front of her blazing home and her DEA husband, who is still inside and dead. What looks like murder may be more heinous as she goes on the run from a group of armed mercenaries. She goes back to her summer job as a fire lookout in a California National Park where she meets the one man who can help her—Jack Widow.

The next book, THE LAST RAINMAKER, pulls Widow out the hospital after a train wreck, where he is discovered by an old frenemy. CIA Agent Tiller wronged Widow in the past in a secret mission to North Korea that got Widow's team killed at the hands of the deadliest sniper who ever lived. Now, Tiller needs Widow's help to stop the same sniper, known as a Rainmaker. The sniper has reemerged taking out his victims from great distances. His target list: the world record holders for longest confirmed kills.

The tenth book that follows is THE DEVIL'S STOP, which refers to all the places in the USA named after the devil like Hellbent, New Hampshire, a small town that time forgot. First day there, Jack Widow meets a beautiful former Air Force MP who's desperately seeking her husband all while being nearly nine months pregnant. Widow being the man he is means that he's got to help. What starts as a simple missing person soon turns deadly when they uncover that the missing husband was involved in a top-secret government nuclear program and the evil team of dishonored mercenaries who are after it.

What are you waiting for? The fun is just starting—once you start Widow, you won't be able to stop!

THE JACK WIDOW BOOK CLUB

Building a relationship with my readers is the very best thing about writing. I occasionally send newsletters with details on new releases, special offers and other bits of news relating to the Jack Widow Series.

If you are new to the series, you can join the Jack Widow Book Club and get the starter kit.

Sign up for exclusive free stories, special offers, access to bonus content, and info on the latest releases, and coming soon Jack Widow novels. Sign up at www.scottblade.com.

THE NOMADVELIST

NOMAD + NOVELIST = NOMADVELIST

Scott Blade is a Nomadvelist, a drifter and author of the breakout Jack Widow series. Scott travels the world, hitchhiking, drinking coffee, and writing.

Jack Widow has sold over a million copies.

Visit @: ScottBlade.com

Contact @: scott@scottblade.com

Follow @:

Facebook.com/ScottBladeAuthor

Bookbub.com/profile/scott-blade

Amazon.com/Scott-Blade/e/B00AU7ZRS8

Printed in Great Britain
by Amazon